Enchanted Lucky Fool

Enchanted Lucky Fool

A collection

Darrell J. Gawlik

Writers Club Press
San Jose New York Lincoln Shanghai

Enchanted Lucky Fool
A collection

Writers Club Press
an imprint of iUniverse.com, Inc.

For information address:
iUniverse.com, Inc.
5220 S 16th, Ste. 200
Lincoln, NE 68512
www.iuniverse.com

ISBN: 0-595-18212-7

Printed in the United States of America

This is for all those who supported, believed and loved. Also, this is for those who didn't.

Contents

Chapter One

I, Weathered Years

A Birthday Wish

Eighteen years of age and I still cry deep down inside, from within my gut, like a child who has lost his mother. I mask the agony in a hole that I have created in my chest. Still, it hurts! Maybe, it's a cry for attention? Maybe it's a cry for direction? Maybe it's my imagination that has peaked to it's fullest and I am ready to drown in all my sorrow?

Questions are what fill my thoughts every waking hour and every breath I take.

Downhearted.

Yes, that's what I believe the psychologist would call my nature.

Depressed.

That's what I call my state. This state has no reason to dwindle in front of my face without giving an answer to my questions. Reasons are not justified within my knowledge, all I feel is the pain; the pain of loneliness, hatred and the fear of being unique. I am not saying I am physically lonely, nor can I feel the warm comforting arms that hold on to me when I am sobbing in the middle of the night. I am mentally deserted.

A loved one can say, "I love you" a hundred times over again, yet my heart and soul will not let the words be filled with meaning. Their words are hollow syllables and filled with grammatical errors. I am numb.

I've been in love before…haven't we all? My heart took a defeat when the angel broke my heart. Here, I am left with fifty rooms of closed doors and vacant hallways; everything is draped in gloom. The skeleton key is buried inside these walls; I pound night after night. Perhaps I am being selfish and refuse to let anyone show me the light through the cracks, since I am comfortable in the darkness. The torch songs are vital and keep my heart beating. They keep me gratified.

Unfair it is to say that I am not in love. Oh Yes! I think I am. Despair and shattered dreams and bleeding hearts are those that I am in love with, not the sunshine and its heated rays. My eyes won't separate, nor decipher the shades of colors that beam through. All I see is gray.

Do I pity myself? NO. Not one individual should look to themselves for sorrow and grief; that's what friends are for. I don't think of myself as an unsympathetic symbol of melancholy. I welcome it all into my small world of disillusions. I am now a fixed stone on the edge of dying cliff, where once I was a flowering bud in the field of dreams.

Hate.

Hate surrounds my being. An aura of self-destruction and demise wrapped into a tiny feature called a smile. Hate harks at my conscious and relieves the guilt of sins passed.

Funny! I can say; "I love you" a million times a day to a million faces poised in my direction looking for acceptance and friendly spirits, yet I don't even love myself! Now, what can of Asshole concept is that? I don't even have the creditability to have those words (I love you) flow from my lips to another person's ears. When those words escape from my mouth they should fall to the ground and be buried under the tracks of my soles.

You might think I am never joyful. I am very joyful, only it's a façade for me to display to others. This is what people expect and I am all for living up to peoples expectations. I hold myself accountable to make sure this little game happens. I am delighted to mystify someone into believing something that is false. Today is not your turn, for I am speaking from the mind of someone that was and wants to be again. I was hoping you could offer some guidance.

I try not to live in a dark shadow. One that has been condemned to be unruly and unsightly for all to see, yet it just happens.

I still live in my castle. A castle that haunts every fiber, of the living, and hinders the acceptance of ones willingness to project their beauty as a human being. Does that make sense? I question you to question yourself. I dare you. My castle is filled with knights and guards protected by sorrow and housed in fear. I am still waiting for the dark stranger to take me away, until the stranger comes I will continue to bury myself in my own grief and hatred. I am my own worst enemy and I thrive on the thrill of being my own ghost.

Tears tend to roll down my face, yet the misery will stain my cheeks leaving its marks of victory. Perchance this is my good-bye and I shall start the ceremony by propping my arms up full length and begin waving my hand in farewell. I am waving good-bye to childhood, adulthood and all those fascinating stages in between. I am also saying adieu to the first part of grief and welcoming the second wind. Here we go again.

This all might sound so depressing and full of self-pity, but it's quite comical. Yes, Humorous. Laugh! Laugh as loud as your voice will carry and bellow from within your loins and burst into tears. For the joke is and always will be on me. The little boy who is confused. Laugh at him as he tried to reach out and grab on to anything and anyone who wants to relief him of his misery and bewilderment. Laugh at him for trying to "fit in". Laugh at him for being unique and weird. Laugh at him for being an individual and venturing out of the realm that has been molded around him. Take back your voices for the boy has given up the fight. The little boy is not up to the challenge of the war between individuality and the melting pot. He gave up on life.

DAMN!

I am different, not saying different is wicked; yet it does hurt. Especially on the days of your eighteenth birthday.

I chuckle.

There for a moment in time, I let a stream line of happiness invade my body. In that stream of fixed emotion I felt as if somebody cared, and they did. It was I. Perhaps that was my self-respect? I haven't visited him in a long time.

A birthday wish.

What shall I wish for? One item only. I wish that I could stop the never-ending wailing and the constant dying of my lesser soul and let the pain break free.

I need to cry.

I need to weep in someone's arms all night and feel that someone weep for me.

A String of Lights

(dedicated to Andrea Green)

Haunted.
Sheltered from your desolate womb.
Can I cry another salted tear?
Shall I burden my skin with the anguish?
Hearing the shouts; "Merry Christmas";
Muffled are the sounds of bells and cheer.
Can the ridges of sanity blanket my body
Lying here on this pillar of mounted cotton?
For my mind is powerful;
Emotions are elevated…
Blood is making noise;
Reflection in my eyes.

I see her.
I feel her in me…
Peaceful
Tranquil is this moment.
I bridge the gap between her and I;
I am her.
I love her;
Therefore she returns her love to me.

Baffled.
Pounding in the midnight air;
I lunge for thoughts;

Hammer in hand.
Plummet for security;
Cord is between my fingers.
Dispersing energy…
Crazed I am.
Trance-like induced…
Something guiding my being.
I want to feel the light;
I want to know Christmas;
I want to see my string of lights.

Exhausted.
Strained beyond repair
I glimpse out the corner of my eye;
Not in mockery,
Approval spread across her face…
I sleep.

Aunt

Reception will be held in the hall, flowers in remembrance of a death
How can we forgive ourselves for shedding tears of laughter?
Poignant in our statements we made, a loss unbearable to witness
White linen draped around a room of hopeless thoughts

The sweetest smile that could turn the rain into rays of sunshine
How you graced lives, kissed a million cheeks
Energy to crack a joke, even when you were spent of your last will
Touched by angels, your voice carried a distinctive message
Faith, love and harmonious capacity of a soul never to be beaten

Yet, in all trials of determination
Of all those who looked to you with adoration and UN-compro-
mised fashion
You have grown weak, your body brittle and worn
A spirit held in the steel cage of your bones, you struggle to breathe
We can only see the woman we once knew, your eyes tell the story

Hands cracked from the stale room, stationary are your legs that
once carried
Breath shorten, a pinched nerve as you exhale from your quarters
"Come on aunt evie, run with the wind" we whisper…
Those words fall short to your ears, only a single heart beat remains

Weeping for a life that offered history and wisdom beyond any that
can comprehend
For I look to the winds for a sign

Enchanted Lucky Fool

In the distance all I see is the one leaf that hangs from the sycamore tree
Holding on for dear life, as the harsh winds brush against it sides
"Let go" I speak ever so softly
As the ray of light blasts through the trees, she is gone

Now we look through picture books, photos old and faded
Of a woman we called friend, wife and mom
You have flown away from our lives....
But not our hearts.

Black Candle

(Dedicated to Am'e)

Many pieces hang from her wardrobe of sarcasm.
Tones and pitches fall from her broad lips, yet everything is graced in
dark crimson.
Things have been left unsaid and love left undone....
She needs no one.
Lifting her brow to the sight of her prey, although she never reveals her
true emotions.
Hiding her feelings in the blues and blacks of the peppermint skies, yet
there is a streamline of men she doesn't touch.
What are her intentions?
Her vehicle stretched in glossy black;
Her nails covered with enamel baked in Dangerous Red;
Hair so black and rich as the thunderclouds that steal the light from the earth.
As she enters the four dwelling walls, nothing but the stench of elegant
perfume and the purest smell of raw leather captivates the audience.
She holds the world in the palm of her two little hands.
Beautiful is her middle name.
Selected individuals know what lurks inside her beating heart. These
individuals see the sunshine that gleams from her radiant brown eyes as
they sparkle when the light shines.
Many see an illusion of heartlessness, bitter coldness and eyes of stainless steel.
Hearing the confident words of praise as she talks with her defiant sylla-
bles using the most perfect nouns, verbs and adjectives.
Some see her as immaculate;
Some see her as a threat.

I see her as a soul.
A soul that is brave with the heart full of courage and with a smile so warm and tender.
Wishful thoughts and promising hope on each star allow me to say...
Thank-You!
You dug in the dirt and believed in I.
Trusted me.
Guided me.
Let the white doves sing your name;
Let the waters grace upon your toes;
Let the world call your name...
BLACK CANDLE!
...As you burn so bright.

Circle

A circumference
Degrees of imagination
Do I tell another story?
Fairy tale dream
Little Jupiter has saved me again,
Penelope leaned on my curtain
Audience fell silent,
Red as Christmas
Honey fell from my lips
I cried out your name.

A circle,
North to south
A fraction undone.
One Undertow;
A dreadful pulse.
A heart weakened in the waves;
Leave me to melt;
Mr. Wonka needs my hands.
I live to watch me die;
For now, I dwell;
In my head, under my eyes
Only for you to see.

Gray obsession

Turn the wheel;
The water is warm;
Melancholy formed in the shape of a heart;
Reflections and perceptions, life to I
Reality is tedious;
Intricate and precise.
Spirits flow, forming the brow of society;
Shepherds place in the calling;
Where are the wolves tonight?
Distinguished and superb;
I wait for the night.
Hollow is thy soul…
Lay the burden to shore;
I have no compass.

Harlot

Beautiful as the rain in May.
She felt as if the honeysuckle;
Immersed in the wrong season.
Therefore, turning her to adamantine.

Can I inquire every intention of every harlot?
Days that seem to vanish;
I close my eyes.

I saw her face once;
A peach nectar;
Woven with sherbet.
Olive eyes;
Semitransparent to the wonders of her world.
A pale face;
White as the snow in December.

Pealing away the clumps of oils;
That hardens the features;
A hidden joy;
Unfound.

She was exquisite.
I loved her;
Only for a moment.
Remembering a somber song;
That I have chosen to forget;

Yet, Recollection came fourth;
Carried into my ears;
Like mother's words of wisdom.

I said Good-bye, Harlot.

Jimmy Jack and Mr. Vodka ˶

Jimmy, Jack and Mr. Vodka have some stories to recount
So he said.
Wondrous times with far off lands and mountains overcastted with
the morning honey dew, a person whom I didn't know
So he remembered.
Places traveled intertwined with journeys unparalleled and too many
nights equivocal, except when you used the starry skies as your map
So he said.
You still lost your way home.
A fountain of youth undiscovered, a spectrum of light came fourth from
your animated grin, yet saddened by the depths of waiting for security
So he said.
Contentment found at the neck of the bottle, longing retrieved at the
bottom, eyes glance east to west in search of another shimmering glass
the upholds temporary euphoria
So he said.
How long does the sweet taste remain?
So he questioned.
As long as there is a fluorescent light blinking in a cool summer's breeze
So he replied.
Aimlessly stumbling with metaphoric slurs he wants someone to nur-
ture his addiction and pull the pain from his chest
So he said.
A heavenly creature wanders these everglades, marshlands and roads
of liberty; still his eyes were lost in the fragrance of strawberry wine
So he said.
A line drawn from the north to the south and south to north, you

traveled as the highwayman. One hand on the wheel and one the glass of deceit.
So he said.

Jimmy, Jack and Mr. Vodka had told their stories. Screwing the cap and drying your lips you lung forward
So he said.
Stable, brilliant and a wiser man stares back into my love ridden eyes
So I said.
Eyes that have cried a thousand oceans and hands that have felt numerous tears looks back at me
So he said.
A past full of experience, triumph and defeats is the person whom I think of everyday
So I said.
Mysteries, darkened rooms and haunted corners lurk in the depths of the unforeseen image still yet to be discovered. You shine a light as a symbol of your trust
So you said.
Feelings left at chance and playing the table with high stakes, I am ready for the deal. Prepared to bare the weight of snake eyes
So I said.
No promise and no guarantee is what is up for the offer with a no return address posted by a picture frame
So he said.
Victory shall be my signature. Wait, Ill write it on your heart.
So I said.
Come rain or may it shine, in the woods there is an old tree where a heart is embedded, that was graced by your touch.
Together, whatever will be,
Will be
We said.

Little Leaf

Little Leaf
Where are you hiding?
Can you still dance with the wind as it blows so fiercely?
Winter is creeping upon your fragile colored body;
Are you afraid?

Little Leaf.
Mother has called the sun in for the fall;
A chill has been placed around your brown edges,
Could I be your shelter?

Little Leaf.
I still remember you swinging under the oak tree as you sang your song
in the summer air.
The air of July was your friend as it breathed life into your little wholesome body. You sat there high up in the tree so proud of your dark and
light greens.

Little Leaf.
I remember you.
So young and naive with no worries in this small world of no perfection,
Do you cry at night when the branches sway in the dark midnight winds?
Do you keep your head held high?

Little Leaf.
I'm scared that you'll go away with the snow and never come back and
visit.

Enchanted Lucky Fool

Maybe you'll write while you're off to the sunset as the snow gently falls
from the heavens,
You might return with the spring.

Little Leaf.
It's time to pack your bags and fall with the autumn breeze.
Remember to write.
Mother knows spring is just a few days away.
Hold on Little Leaf and float.
Float so gracefully to the ground and rest your little head upon mother
earth's beautiful soil.
It's time to become one.

Little Leaf,
Where are you hiding?
The snow is deep and the weather is bitter cold.
The world covered in white drifts and the trees are holding their heads
in sorrow,
I think there'll all crying for you...
I know I am.

Little Sister

Little sister, my how you have grown;
Butterfly, as elders would speak;
Bean pole, I would reply.
Bones so tiny and brittle;
Steal and strong are your words.
Years have gone by;
All I can say is…
Little Sister, my how you have grown.

Lost faith

Fame came too late,
For I started too early.
Reds and blue's used to shine from the rafters;
Now all is pale yellow.
My voice used to flow;
Even the sparrows loved the tunes;
Pitches, tones;
Flat, rejected;
This is a reflection.

Mirror, mirror don't I hate to look at thee;
Wondering.
Wondering what the world looks like from success;
Not face down in an empty can.
Fortune tellers;
Jezebel's;
They all have the same message for me;
Head for the stars;
Forgotten to tell about the curves.

Changing places;
Mirrored faces;
And desolate times ahead.
Dust bowl is the feast.
Challenging time with wits;
Only to see the wrinkles marching.

Darrell J. Gawlik

Once was beautiful;
Goddess like;
Olive skin;
My aura was a fresh picked daisies;
No stature so erect;
And poised for;
Perfection.
Vitamins, minerals swept through the veins of this body;
Energy, life and hope pumping through this vessel;
Majestic places;
Chiseled faces;
Elegance painted from head to toe.

I lay in this bed,
Gasping for each and every breath.
Courage to wake;
Strength to open my eyes.
As I look to my mirror;
Hoping that this reflection would change.
Torn.
Turning from the view;
Losing ground;
Lost faith.

Lost, I am

Hush
Taunting bells,
Can you hear?
Remorse
Fusion of will against power
Someone help

Guilty
Mistaken identity
Greed has its price
Which hand was dealt?
Emaciated
Body stricken
Mind is dumb

Pay the price
Success has failed me
Push toward the light
Falling inward
Forgot the code
Lost, I am

Mona Lisa's Smile

Mona Lisa hasn't smiled in years;
Since they colored her cheeks blue;
Tracing tears around her lips.
Out in the parallel rain;
Mona Lisa's colors faded.
Blues and greens no longer feature her wit;
Yet, leave her lonely and hard-featured.

Mona Lisa;
You color me in midnight blue;
Pea green;
As my demise cries out for assistance.
Stranded in a hollow cube;
A sunset photo in black and white.
Peace between my head and heart;
I couldn't support.
I am ready to locate my children;
They are buried between the pages;
Pages covered in my confession;
Self wit.
Acquiescence to the monastery church of your heart;
Your inner self;
Selfishness blankets my blessing.

An arrowhead slips from a pocket;
Sacrifice my own blood for you;
Crimson red is my beloved color.

Enchanted Lucky Fool

I taste freedom from my misdeeds;
Identify is finally provoked.

I am Mona Lisa's smile;
Exception;
I had a beating heart;
Washing my canvas clean.

Mourn

Dense with theory
...thoughts scramble
justified is my nature

ignorant to the touch
...a lapse history
the future before you and I were stale.

Ripened fields of showering fruits
.... displayed for your engagement,
Lilies, lilacs and poppy fields
...tumble through the weeds
you once were a child.

Eden's garden of purity
...shelter of April's rain
bliss rang the bells
...you captured my heart,
The wind still calls your name.

Admiring your photo
...fingerprints translusive
Fragrance of your body, in the mist
...smoky eyes, curled lips
Say good night tomorrow,
...I only live for today.

Mute

Thunder began to rage
You touched me
I shudder.
You touched me, again
I tremble.
My mind goes frail
Not able to voice.
What I feel, you ignore
What I think, you despise
Who I am; you disregard.

Closing my eyes;
You touch me
I shriek
Touching me, again
Frozen.
Losing myself
Insecure in my own skin
I lye there and stare.
Clouds, rain and bitterness sweep over the bed…
Absent within the thunder
Striking me with your lightening…
Dark with fear
How my knees can bend
Terrified to challenge your intellect
I question why?
Why, at a merciful age?

Pray.
Eyes transfixed in perplexing confusion
Stationary.
Wanting to drown you out
You touch me.
Utter stillness.
Kissing my lips…
Repulsed.
You kiss me, again
He just doesn't know;
He just doesn't comprehend;
Game he is playing…
Is sin.

MYSTERY

Hear the rain as it pours from the sky
Can you feel the freedom?
The wetness funnels around your eyes
Just as a vanilla chocolate swirl

Rain mixing with the salt that fell from your cheeks
Let the water wash your fears away
Let the sun brighten your halo
The one you keep hid.

There's a fountain of gold behind a personality
A treasure that awaits your presence
A dream that you never have dreamed
A wish that you never thought would come true

Feeling the guilt of wasted years
No regrets
A learning experience that will last a life time
The clock is ticking

Saddle up the horses, the wind is blowing north
Fell the cool breeze as you let go of the reins
Freedom isn't in a bottle
Freedom is reality
Not a perception.

I hear your inner child calling out
Suffocate if you will
Yet, the fire is still burning
Free the dustbowl of sorrow

A liquid café is calling
Sit down and breathe
For the fast pace of your soul
Will hinder your heart.

I'll speak to you with comfort
Listen with precaution
For a bond of friendship will not be torn
For only will grow stronger

I look to you
A pillar that holds the mountains
A dam that holds the sea
Dry the tears
Look into the mirror
And smile
For you are loved.

Navy Blue

Sail away from home;
Chosen to play a man;
A sea is waiting.
As you dream your dreams through others;
You obey.
Picture Perfect, a consolation in his head
You wear Navy blue.

Honored, Proud and admirable;
I often stare in bewilderment.
Outbound, overcome and betrayed;
A heart as soft as the gentle snow that falls.
A Sahara;
A wondrous spirit;
Forgiving texture, aristocratic

Features embedding in America's history;
Splendid,
An honor that does not judge;
Longing for forgiveness.
You wear Navy Blue.

Grace,
Fallen upon your eyes;
Nature awaits your voice.
Stroll along the path..
I too, will follow.

Darrell J. Gawlik

A heavenly brilliance;
When you wear,
Navy Blue.

New Tide

Below the bridge
Above the sea
A voice
Calling me

In a dream
Forbidden touching ground
In our hearts
Safe
And sound

Until someone
Breaks a heart
Turning to stone
Left in the midst
Eternal to roam

It's like a daydream
Real as the winter
Real as they may seem
Like wool, on a summer's day
Pants without a seam

New tide, wait for me
We are both heading out to sea
New tide, wait for me
In my dreams
Is where I want to be.

One Day

Lipstick smeared across her lips
Deteriorating light in her eyes,
Straining to see a representation
None of which his her own.

Facades have been arranged,
Truth lined in the blackness of her eyeliner
A soul hidden by pollution of her peers,
No beacon in the twilight
Northern star has revolutionized gray

No strength to muster,
A mirror sheltered with pictures
For a face of agony she masks.

Dim lit rooms, she makes her home
Foliage has turned brownish yellows
No water trickles from her faucets,
Her place of dwelling,
stale as her heart

If only she didn't play that song…
If only she didn't breathe against his skin
If only his stroke didn't grow cold….

Living a life of seclusion
Hair is turning gray, frayed years of abandonment

Enchanted Lucky Fool

Wedding band embedded in her finger,
No white circle is seen.

Overlooked words that once were uttered
Dialogue that is left, hushed away
A melodrama in her head

She will say adieu…. One day
She will say farewell……. One day
She will say adios……….One day
One day might nevermore come again.

Path and Gate

A path of seduction;
A path worn with thorns;
Insects armed;
Stench of hormones.
Lilacs draped;
Remembrance;
Hovering the entrance.
In those who pass through;
Of those who passed.
Pebbles engrave "welcome home";
Dirty hands;
Deceitful minds;
Pleasures of unforeseen desires;
Plague a path and gate.
A brook overflows with sin;
From the bodies that have been laid.
Souls turn from the path;
Families await their love and dedication.
Repressing their actions;
Another sun will await their presence;
Their footprints will linger in the mud.
Wandering down seduction;
A path and gate.

Pocket girl

(Dedicated to Ann Kirkwood)

A pocket girl;
One broken heel, wings at her side;
Standing in mid-flight,
Standing alone,
A face painted in the wind;
Admire her.

A pocket girl;
Chose your words judiciously;
For a lady in disguise;
And a child at heart;
Paint yourself a gentleman;
Admire her.

A pocket girl;
Spoken in harsh tones;
Underlying her concerns;
Bats her eyes
Hearts will fall;
Admire her.

A pocket girl;
Specific to the point,
Mocking carelessly;
Provoking hysterical laughter;

Moved to be at her side;
Admire her.

A pocket girl;
A face of perfection;
A smile of diamonds;
A heart of beautiful words;
A woman anyone could count on...
I admire her.

Pretty Girl

Pretty girl, statuesque.
Mold her into a victim of your triumph;
Suppress the golden ideas with your icicle wisdom.
Staying afloat on the hit parade,
Your charm overpowers, while delusive on the inside;
You suffocate a dreamer.
Question that needs sought;
Not pinned a destination.
For now,
I consider my vacancy of life;
A reservation that has been planned.
They have entitled myself in the world;
I am filed under the chapter,
Lost.

Red Balloons

Candy hearts and red balloons is what I should feel;
Blue skies and crimson rain, cool breezes is what I should view;
Where are all the fountains of gold that I search for?
How do I find the mysteries that I yearn to have?
I can hear the soldiers entering my mind;
The rattling of the guns;
The shiny brass bullets are armed inside their coats;
Fear does not overwhelm my being;
Only the loneliness that is subsided in my body.
Love surrounds my life;
Why then, does nothing enter my mind? A question that baffles
my intellect.
Roses are in full bloom, yet no mystery unfolds.
The smoke hasn't cleared;
Therefore my eyes fumble to see the beauty.

I smile with a façade that acquaintances can not tear through;
In a phone booth with no communicative devices;
This is how I see my life.
I want not, so I read in a book of knowledge;
I do want, I hear from my heart.
Looking to the trees for comfort,
I find myself embedded in the bark;
My name in scribed, chiseled into the pulp of tomorrow.

Pictured is the smiles and laughter I once known;
Who was to tell me I would falter?

Living and learning;
I do not teach myself.
Books of lines, all black and steel;
I find my way home again.
Once a little boy in mother's arms;
Now a man at the mercy of the world;
I smile at the memory, not the metaphors;

I could lie to myself,
Say that I am clean.
Dust in my eyes;
Trying to see the beauty in humans.
A sweet song of sorrow;
A song of the sea.

Some Contemplations

I.   When foundation has been laid;
       A heart fills with salty tears;
       The power of love can not be denied.

II.   Waterfalls haul my anguish;
       I linger in the colors;
       I shall carry my grief elsewhere.

III.   Excuse me God.
       But I want to go;
       I want to live up in the heavens;
       Although everyone tells me no.

       Life on earth has no reason;
       It only changes seasons.

       So, if you don't mind, God;
       I want to die...
       Like an eagle;
       Take me;
       I want to fly.

SUGAR SUGAR

Sugar Sugar
Where are you?
Lost in the midst of the wind
Sugar Sugar
Where are you?
Lost in the vines of the angry men

A story so promising
A story so profound
A twig in your hair
Golden locks on the ground

Can u see in the afterglow?
Face and name unheard
Can hear the sirens blow
Sugar Sugar chimes the bird

Silently crept and wept on your back
Thoughts replaced
Mexico, they're unattached

Dreams of candy canes and mysteries galore
True identity misplaced
Who are they and what for?

Darrell J. Gawlik

Sugar Sugar
Where are you?
Sugar Sugar
....I am still blue.

Survive

How do I survive?
Endless, is this world;
Revolving around my crown,
Orchids falling to my feet.
Is this bliss?

The fortune cookie

How precise the edges have been cut
Not by man, nor machine
Something legendary is affixed
Why a fortune printed in black or red lettering?
Why one's destiny on such snow white paper?

Eagerness displayed in a room of tacky greens
Prissy purples and blanched pinks,
The relentless task of eating
A goal in each individual eyes
Get the main course, the mid course, the dessert
Anxiously awaiting for the mute waiter
Arrived
Ahhhhh…at last
The fortune cookie.

Static of the silence, overbearing in contrast
Eating in harmonious teething bites
Saving the fortune cookie for last,
A slight tear in the black ink
Destiny a waits
Nervousness rooted from the stems of curiosity,
Beautiful, fragile and whitish brown crispy
Sugar fix in right hand
Left hand gently pulling
Gravity holding it down
Pieces scatter around the flat white table

Enchanted Lucky Fool

Fortune in hand
Threats in mind
Your future has succumbed to those of a factory

How do you eat your fortune cookie?

The Man on Wayne Street

I could see behind the eyes;
They burned with innocence.
Desire was between the lines;
That he had spoken.

Habitat was picturesque;
Knickknacks of sorts;
Culture was prominent.
Moons and stars ornamented from his sky;
He's a dreamer.

Excitement filled the room;
Anticipation was null.
Did you dare to venture into my wounds?
A surface shown to him;
Without reservation.

Wondering eyes;
Minus the touch.
Hands to the side;
Space confined.
Did you want my skin fronting your skin?

Questions instilled in my mind;
A soul that searches.
For I am a the most content;
In solace.
I dare not question my motives.

Apprehensive.
Gentle winds blow through the curtains;
Rain falls in my chest.
Decisions provoked;
Actions not surrendered.
I search myself.

Wayne Street;
A fantasy left unsorted;
The hunt ceased.
Could you find the potency;
To hold your gaze?
I wanted to inquire.

Crazed.
Parallel lives;
Two way streets;
The city burns of cowards.
For I see the child;
In your beautiful eyes.

Stepping foot from door to street;
Never once to return.
Finding myself;
At the foot of your stairs;
Once again.

Darrell J. Gawlik

Has your life been easy?
A doubt;
That lingers.
Tough.
A façade that you betray.
Yet, I know you.

No horoscope gave you away;
Fortune tellers;
Not in sight.
I knew you…
When I met the man on Wayne Street….
One night.

These Are Moments

Lightening crosses the sky;
Rain falls gently on my face.
Raincoat slightly snug;
Wool graces my cheeks.
These are moments I live for.

Blades of grass under my feet;
Sun warms my body.
Wind blowing through my hair;
A smile.
These are moments I live for.

Family memories spread across the floor;
Faded photographs on my lap.
Black and white in years untold;
Color reflects recent age.
These are moments I live for.

Flowers dangle in the dirt;
Hands soiled from the earth.
Butterfly's dangle around my head;
A reflection in the rim of a bicycle.
These are the moments I live for.

Crimson, blush and forest;
Sky painted on a canvas.
Water ripples against the sandstone;

Brushing up against my toes.
These are the moments I live for.

Darkness falling around my shoulders;
Hands clutched, mouths conversing
Standing erect in devastation, you and I…
There are moments I live for.

Mother calling;
Inquisitive about daily practices.
Grandma telling;
Everything is in love.
These are the moments I live for.

Turn on the radio;
Love songs playing all day long.
Dancing and singing;
Forgetting the daily hassles;
These are the moments I live for.

Lemon pie, sugar cookies and chocolate chips;
Bake while we sing.
Smell of family in the air;
Everyone shares each other's victories
These are the moments I live for.

Fiction and lies;
Instilled in my head.
I cry;
For my imagination played tricks on me.
Those were the times I would've lived for.

Time

Tick and tock;
Wood hands grasping for space;
Running from the past;
Only to find the future at hand;
Devastated, depressed.
Turmoil in my palm;
I lay here to rest.

UNDER THE PEDALS

Funny.
I don't shock you by the way my lips move.
Piercing.
My voice carries down the hallway to the boys that laugh. I figured I could fit in with the boys, therefore I shunned emotions. Can I make one more mistake?
Forgiven.
I never say, "sorry."
Too many words for an emotion, that I don't care to feel. You might say that I am cold. You might even say that I am hard on those that I love.
Correct.
I turn my blue sky upside down, for I like to see the birds fall to the ground
Confused.
I feel wicked when someone puts his or her head on my shoulders. They feel that I am stronger than they are. Cowards they are to be so naïve. How dare they look to me as a pillar in the night or when they have lost their soul.
No remorse.
I am not bitter. I am jealous of spirit that flows through other humans. How can they be so humble and content? My mind wonders three thoughts per every two seconds.
Illusions.
I like the snow. Bitter and cold is what I can relate too. I yearn for the snow to melt and create the devastating floods. It runs through my blood and father time never was my friend.

Underestimated.

Solitude has always been there by my side. Home is just a word for regrets and loneliness. I unveil to you the truth, as I perceive it. I look at the world through my smoke filled eyes and feel the warmth of the sun through a vile.

Destructive.

Under the pedals, just my emotions and my home away from home. No one can tell me what is right and wrong Under the Pedals. I do love; I love when everything is wrong. I am just made up of surfacing facades and lies.

Welcome to my home…

Under The Pedals.

Up-Close

Look into the mirror;
Frowns form;
Muscles contract;
Age is apparent in the frame.
Smiles, I haven't seen in days.
Remove the scratches in the photo;
A glimpse of contentment.
A lie is formed.

Morals and values conflict in an aging skull;
Appearance is worth monetary value;
A reflection of skin and bone;
Persecution is the white-winged dove
On a blistering winter's morning.
For I can not feel the warmth of the sun,
Feeling the bitterness of rejection,
Dwelling in the sanctuary of perverse action;
I stem only my grief to those surrounded.

Bitterness has weighed upon my heart;
A superficial river made only from finest ingredients:
Consternation, disallowance, and loathing;
Do you dare to come forth with your cloak
Of appetite?
Dismantle verses appreciation;
Tell of your story.

I hang my head in bewilderment;
Thought I retrieved a kindred spirit; yet
My representation in this mirror proves
My evidence as insubstantial.
I loathed viewing my face;
I grieve at my photograph;
I bellow for guidance.
Satisfied with my conclusions,
Restoration is in order;
Only when affection enters my dorm;
Hatred subsides;
And I raise my head in fondness,
Of what I see in the mirror;
Looking back at me.

Wavering Greed

Buttons, laces and a delicate smile;
Fingernails lined with gold.
Wholesome cheeks;
Dotted pinks in perfection you admire.
Ears laced with diamonds,
Nose powdered to the nines;
Observing an exhale
From across the room.

Fashioned in pearls,
Drenched in hatred, sarcasm pours
From your skin.
Eyes burn in laser lines,
Words taunt.
Whipping your black mane,
As the ice scatters upon
Your shoulder.

Men dazzle;
Women scorn.
Tormenting the weak;
Feasting on the hungry.
A lady of wealth,
Demising the commons.

Remember who you are,
Superstar.

Chapter Two

Art of Melancholy

Memory

The moon is full;
Tides are high
A single tear down my cheek;
Remembering your face.

Letters compile your absence;
Text a can not see;
Photograph creased with years;
A press to my heart.

Time will heal my wounds;
For your farewell was my defeat;
Floating with the leaves
Winter is upon my heart.

A couple last words before I start to cry;
Here's a toast to you, Good-bye.

Anguish

Anguish.
Black coal streaked across my face
Eyes once burned evergreen
Turn of a dime
Burdened with gray
Rose red were my lips
Parted equally with a smile
You speak, I hush
Sewn eternally as one
Stationary
Two hands, I signal a good-bye
One heart, I let fracture
As you drift from my life

Arrivederci

Mother is quarreling among herself;
It doesn't comfort my thinking, anymore;
Thrashing, screaming
Tongue-tied and belligerent
Joy has turned to suffering.
Interpret reasoning, I shun the answer
Grasping a solution;
I've been bitterly isolated;
In the depths of your perception.

Fairy tales and sugar coated plums;
I dance in my mind;
Pink Elephants, beckoning my concentration;
Tranquillity, is limited
Sorrow escalated.
I defuse linked emotion.

Troubled heart,
Swelling in my chest.
Vision blurred around the edges;
I wipe the tears.
Must carry onward;
Voices I hear calling me.

Prairies all awaiting my presence;
Mother earth awaits a torn soul.
Mother, still thrashing and screaming..

Images embedded in my head;
Endless years.
Although, her voice carries bells…
Reminding me each time I think;
Even after I had buried her.

Perceive input, no long optioned;
My love has carried away;
Motionless is my virtue;
You're a sin I wear
For I loved you.

I wait.
Bitterly patience as the sun sets;
The dawn, laughing;
Poking fun at my misfortune.
I waver no choice;
I surrender;
Hate and ill luck
Become my home.

Arrivederci…Mother;
Arrivederci…Voices;
Arrivederci…the dawn;
Open arms… Deceased.

Center Stage

Preparing the backdrop
You center stage
What made me think I could win this time?
Lights stationed for your entrance
I hide behind the curtain
As he watches from the wings
You tremble to give your speech
I fall short of breath
He breathes deep as he prays for your answer
Holding the manuscript
Torn between what and what not to do
The audience is overwhelmed with anticipation
I slowly take a seat in the balcony
Realization is taking over
For your eyes are heavy
Heart beat exhilarating
I see your tremble
He waits for you
His knees filled with anxiety
A heart pouring out for another chance
I look to him
Nodding with encouragement
'Tis all I have to give
Sweat pouring from your glands
Not able to voice
The audience held captive
I, will always be here

I will cheer for the words you do not speak
Prompt you for the lines you forgot
He's changed as he waits
You've changed as you ponder
I just need to let you go
I shall not leave your presence, just alter my intentions
For I still am near
Yet only watching from the balcony
No longer behind the stage
You whisper your lines
Vague as they may be
You understand
He understands
I already know.

Conversation

Writer0319: *Can you please find my heart?*
I imagine I left it back at the crossroads,
Intersections failed and forgotten
If you're not able to help me
Then can I borrow a piece of love from yours?
I promise to give it back when mine returns home...

Writer0319: *Hidden in Deep Crevasses*
A hole merely without depth
Yet, captured by the realm of perception
I search
I stumble
Rocks and mountains shun my victory
Still, I cry in the night...
Heart, Be Found!

Miacat3: *How can I tell you*
My heart is your heart
And pieces are never enough
No heart is lost
Merely hidden
For moments
Yours...perhaps here with me

Darrell J. Gawlik

Writer0319: **Written by Darrell Jackson Gawlik**
Miacat3: *Written by Deborah Wright*

Could I Be...

My eyes are heavy;
My heart is weak.
Mindless actions result in careless ideas;
What more do you want from me?

I search my steps;
For the stones I stumble;
I am back where I started.
No beginning, nor conclusion;
I leave my body in shambles.

I dread the sun;
I worship the night.
For in darkness we are all the same.
Ideas have vanished in the dusk;
I yearn for knowledge;
I just fall behind.

Old man winter came upon my soul;
Cold and brittle are my words;
May you warm me with your breath?
I hold onto the steel;
My hands falter.

Love is what I fear;
Desolate is my self-worth;
Foreigner to the lines you speak.

Covert; that I am.
Cowardliness runs in my blood;
Don't scorn my appetite.
For that is all I have left.

Remain in the corner;
Parallel with my figure.
Shadows dare not intersect;
For I will capture your light sneeze.
Live no more.

Continue my path of destruction;
I beg, not your pity;
But forgiveness.
Tortured in my own world;
Faith is no more.
Touch my skin;
You burn.
Candles surround your presence;
I blow you out.
Could I be...
More vulnerable?

Dead, Confused

When pain hollows out your soul;
You're dead.
When sorrow pleads, the verdict
Devastated conclusions;
You're dead.
When suffering subsides,
Loneliness prevails;
You're dead.
When tear stains fade,
A face so cold;
You're dead.
When spirit drifts;
A winter song unsung;
You're dead.

I've no more pain.
I've no more sorrow.
I've no more suffering.
I've no more tears.
I've no more spirit.

Why am I not dead?

DEAR STRANGER

Dear Stranger,

Take one look at my face, my lines, creases and the paleness that does not shine anymore. I am not the light that will make your day grow brighter, nor am I the person who can make your dreams come true. Unfortunately, I am just another person breathing the same stale air that carries each one us along our empty days. I see the hope in your sway as you linger across the room to greet, with a sturdy handshake and a swift hello. The smoke fills the room and my eyes water from the true delight of you noticing my boy like features. Yet, I am underlined in gray and sadness fills these clothes that hang from my bones. There are things that I see in your face that I will not be able to help you erase nor rewind.

I can not release your anger that has been buried for years, nor can I help you resolve what your daddy did to you. I can lend an ear once in awhile and sometimes I pat on the back. I can not lend you a shoulder, for mine is brittle and is worn. The strength once fused in my stride as been burned and I have grown weak. Therefore I will not be able to carry you home when your heart has been beaten and the world pounding you to the walls. I am not courageous anymore. I only can watch from afar to make sure you don't slip on the ice that you tread.

I have been searching for that someone to stand by me; when I am crushed to the floor with an ocean of tears before my eyes. I know you think you can find tranquillity in my embrace, peace between my fingertips. Yet, these hands are chapped from the harsh cold words that I have caught between the truths and lies of fellow men.

My body is warm with blood from the heat of my heartbeat. When you touch me, the heat you feel is from the pain that I am hiding and the scars that never seem to heal.

You say I looked like an angel from across the room with a smile that captured your soft glance. You continue to speak of my eyes that burn like a thousand candles and how my skin smells so sweet. As I blush from the brilliant lines that you have spoke, I shun away from your hope filled eyes. You know not the secrets that dwell inside these veins and the past that has laid its finger-prints upon my body. The eternal cold winter night does not fade when summer peers his head; he has found a place inside my soul. I am captive in this never-ending bind of inadequacy.

Stranger, for I am just an empty well, a fountain made of rock and stone, having no life to offer. I have been traveling this blessed earth for 25 long years and still stumbling on my own two feet. I guide with my intuition and have found a pot of nothing lingering over my head, which hangs so delicate and low. My legs are made of lead, while my arms are shattered wings.

Wandering aimlessly and destined to search for another hope-less dreamer; I will carry my values in my pocket and my morals around my waist. Underneath the sky, the smell of spring drift-ing against my hair, I shall continue on my journey of a quest of self-destruction. One day will be filled with content and true overbearing joy and balloons around my wrists. That shall be the day that true love knocks me over with a soft whisper and a beautiful hello.

So, I might seem to be a perfect guy under all the lights that shimmer, but I am just a mere lad striving to find my way back home, while trying to mend this broken heart.

Different Shades

Thinking,
Perplexed in many angles
Nudging the thoughts

On a broken window sill
Rain brings the message
A vow that will be kept true
Undisputed
Nothing slips off the tongue
Whispering sorrows

Forgotten tomorrow's
I now fear life
In different shades

Feel So Different

A gentle breeze;
Kindred spirits.
How does hope dissolve?
A wheel and some string…
Paying the price of solitariness.
I still dream.

Leaving home, a wanderer…
No beacon in the night.
Caress my palms, touch my lips;
Colorless and gray…
I still dream.

Let my guard fade;
Whisper your name
Say good-bye
Liberty.

Forgotten, I am

Forgotten, Is a day of pleasure
Intrigue darkened with plague
Isolated in frozen tongue
Circled by a wrath
Haunted with remorse
A hand that fed,
A hand severed.
Does faith still believe in me?
A path of rotten fruit, a stolen crown
Forgotten, I am.

After Glitter Fades

The curve of his chin, razor edged jaw line
Vividly recollecting how prominent we fit for three years
Our torso's touched
Hands clenched
Lips graced each other with vitality and passion
Reflections of our youth
Endless nights drawing attention to the sun setting
While love carried us onward
We were dreamers
Mine yours, yours mine
In the distance, we fell behind

We've covered up deceit while the wallpaper hides the stains
Tears in the mattress of which we lay
You have found tranquillity in dreams
While I lay wide-awake in deep slumber thought

Dusk falls
Loneliness creeps in through the windowpane
Desolate hunger
I starve for what you do not offer

I decorate our kingdom in floral of vibrant colors,
While you paint in blacks and grays
The china has begun to chip
Streaks of color run down the walls.

Slipping into haze, raining days resemble sympathy
Yet, I continue to fight your isolation
Screaming in the corners of my mind
SPEAK to me as your lover
KISS me as if your worldly possession
HOLD me as you would your own child
For I am flesh and blood
With a heart that beats only for you

Weeping as I call your name…
"WHERE ARE YOU?!"
Am i strong enough to crawl deep inside
and pull out your rage?
Or am I weak enough to have just settled?
Conditions beyond ability to regulate
Patiently, I wait.

Love letters still pour from my body onto paper,
Paper that is lined with your name,
Signing "with love."
With each movement of my pen,
A drop of tenderness flows with the ink in which I write….
Even after the glitter fades.

Hand

My hand wide open to the world;
Heart vise by the shore.
Only reveal what the man saw;
I was young.
The creases of the palm imprinted;
My shoulder is heavy;
I want to cry.
No being here;
Alone.
I open my hand;
Here, now, is my palm;
Can you still feel me?

Intensity

Lay me down where the flowers die
Can you feel the poison running through your veins?
Your eyes, like a two way glass,
Pour mystery into my life.
I live for your breath, is it right
I said
Is it right?
You said.

Two seconds and a minute pass;
I look to your picture,
Wanting to tear it in half,
Your harmful.
Yet, I yearn for each and every touch.
A warm sensation tingles my stomach,
Placing your claws onto my skin,
I crave you, intensely.

Razor sharp, your tongue pushed through my lips,
Hearts racing, two blocks left.
I know why the birds all sing.
Your words keep whispering.
Tide is high and my faith is low,
I burned the books,
And kissed your face.
Can you feel the strength in my touch,
I can't fall in love.

Enchanted Lucky Fool

Temptations is at it's peek,
Dilate the front,
Give back your key,
One more word,
A whisper left in the wind....
Your heart beat, when mine was broken.
It's time to go.
It's time to grieve.

Intrigued

You have caught me;
Victim, I am.
Riding the horses;
For, no coach wants to carry me.
Falling to my knees;
I dismiss pride.
Looking away into the distance;
I once loved you.

Jealously

Tunnel vision, limbs smoldering
Scent of isolation, haunting bones
Beneath the canopy…
Draped vines, seductive fruits, succulent raspberries
I taste the wine.

Liquid surface, rocks between my toes
Drifting sand, you close my eyes
Dreaming, color's harmonious
I touch the sky.

Fall behind, nowhere to be seen
Walls so thick, space divides
Mustard paint, granny smith apple green tints
Diving, belly first
I forgive.

She, with desire triggered
Unfastened buttons, tie the lace
Underworld Goddess, awaken
Claws of venom, mouth of deceit
Go with her, I lie.
Façade takes shape, you lie.
Deep waters…
Who's left standing?

Hands lose grip, tears fall
Lifeline vanished, a wrinkle appears
Terrible hours, bitter pain
Lifeless joy, I wait.
A moment dies, visions deceptive
Summer rain sheds it's skin, open my eyes
Looking down, a puddle
...and my reflection.

Luna

Chasing turtledoves through the winter reminds her of time when life was kind and the roof had no leaks. She would sit and color all day by the fire; nobody told her she was wrong. She'd dance with lazy curls in her hair and never glance twice at the material she wore.

Simplicity,

Letters scrawled in the dirt of a place she would someday venture off to, never in her mind a neither doubt nor if. Visions of candy canes and fruit filled her blood shot eyes; she someday would be queen. Holding the power of struggle and happiness in the palm of her hand...she would giggle.

Silent and delicate was she. Never knowing for one moment to the other, yet loving herself the same. Questions that had no answers ever touched her mind.

She was perfection.

She was the hourglass that the sand of time would never run out of, and she could see for miles with no fog in sight.

Turmoil and demise passed her with lucky bouncing back and fourth, yet she would never give up. She would sing in whispered tongue and talk with the angels standing by.

She had friends.

Pick the daisy.

Smell the rose.

Which would you want to be?

The called her Luna.

Slam the door; close your eyes...are you in heaven again? Drink your water and put your hand to your mouth.

She's not ashamed.

She has love and forgiveness in her own little sanctuary. She needs no one else. Boys would enter her forbidden place of desire, yet she would show them to the door. They all saw her image of self-destruction and hatred.

Running through the strawberry fields and hiding in green meadows she would bow down to the grave sight of a lonely old man. Luna would dance and sing at this spot of preconceived death. She was content as long as the moon was out with the midnight sun and the sun was out with the blue spangled sky. She would recall of past lives and ancestors that have haunted her little soul.

She loved stories.

Luna didn't hate.

She disliked.

She had the ability to turn the situation of uncommon ground and compile it into a pond of melted chocolate and crystal waterfalls.

Passing through the under ground she would whistle in silence. She never cared for the Christian boys, nor did she like the rocks that filled her mind.

Twisted.

Her mind complex with the thought of a purple plum with no seed; is this what she felt inside?

Luna never cared for love,

She had pride.

Sometimes she would venture off to the bookstore looking for the pages of an empty magazine. Filling the blank pages with her fairy tales and visions of skepticism.

Looking onward through life's little window she would bow her head down and let the tears flow from her dark sunken eyes. Mascara would run down her cheeks seeping into her frail lips.

She would whisper the name of her mother. The person who never left the light on; the only one she believed in was gone.

Memories are left in her vacant mind as she dreamed.

Dreams so vivid and clear. She was running to the stream of hope. She knelt down and looked into the water of reflections. There she would see her mother's eyes in the crystal stream. No one was able to understand. They all just called her Luna with no judgment in their hearts, or did they?

She longed for her mother as she remembered when her mother would cradle her in her arms. Life has changed and all alone Luna stands her ground. Chocolate ponds and crystal waterfalls won't exist anymore. She hangs her head over the pond of hope and realizes there are no answers.

Luna.

Why did she venture down to that stream everyday? Why would she dance with lazy curls in her hair in the fields of endless sky?

The white limousine pulled up; two people entered the room. The smell of roses lye all around and her face so pale and still. Her mother's head hung down in shame as she asked her self-the rolling questions that once ventured into Luna's head. They buried Luna in her sundress that she wore in the poppy fields.

Her mother wondered down to the stream where the answers would lye. The stream now filled with mud and rocks, no trace of Luna's passion for life.

The sun set and rose for you.

Luna,

No one could enter that world of solitude that you secretly held for yourself. No one could vision the world through the window such as you did. You took the life of the poppy fields and the streams of hope with you.

It was all for you...Luna.

Malaise

Trickle down the back;
Feeling the voice plague your soul,
A dread of words
A repulsive action,
Questions arise
Answers fall!
Under the weather
A sea of sorrow,
Shall I dive in?
Captain Ahab would undermine authority;
Disgrace upon his face,
I am captured in a delusion.
Tolerate,
A word that unsuitably describes my presence…
A somber song in the wind
I am wholesome!
I am a forgettable!

Ode to a lover

Captions in a life where deaf only lead, I meant

A world of intangible wonders. I shall not lead
You, but follow.
Cracks in a sidewalk, turning sideways to steal
A glance. Weeping Willow stifles the words that
I am longing to convey.
Tracing, painting or smearing thoughts, hopeless
As the angel standing over the tombstone.
Inadequate disbelief surrendered to the villains,
In my head.
Steering an auto with no headlights, oblivious to
The lines painted ahead, declaration in hindsight
Why must I fester with incomplete sentences?
Unparalleled grammar along side, the stumble in
My stride.
Eminent occasion scarred in a pool of doubts
Study the curve of his brow, as I remember
When you spoke of love.

Picture

Creases in the paper; no edges
Are torn.
Lips are faded; faces unknown;
Could I have loved this fiber;
Everything is aching and torn.

Burning the image; not erased from my mind;
Salty drops stream down from my lids;
My lips curl from the sound of your
Laughter from long ago,
I drop the picture....
And let go.

Pictures in my Head

Fumbling Towards the Infinite ground that held me to you;
In a sea of tranquillity that led me to your soul.
Where is the deep green ocean where I lay down my defense?
Open the portals that shall reveal a bittersweet heaven.
What do I represent to you?

A mockingbird in the distant sings a song of love and hate;
Where do I perch my heart?
Snow has drifted all around my forbidden desire of you and I.
The ice has covered my heart with the breeze of the morning winds;
Do I return
In your arms of peacefulness?

Clouds of rain have vanished where the tide has meant the shore;
Merely a symbol of wholeness.
Yet, I feel empty and filled with the sorrowful regret.
Will you come to shelter me in this shower of hate?
I spare little kindness and cast my emotions into a pool of dust.
Wanting you to haunt my black veil of winter.
I surrendered.

Rag Doll

Heart shaped face
Hollow marble eyes
Aftermath of pain.
Life doesn't exist for the rag doll.
Color is only a dream.
Limber.
Flexible.
Time is a virtue, only left to be unseen.
He doesn't feel the loneliness the surrounds him;
Comprehension is desolate.
I see a little of him....
In me.

Sail

Forecast summons winds from the northeast; guess I won't count on my sail today. Blue oil paint streaks have been spilled against my canvas of unwritten inspirations. I still harbor the anticipation of your glance and cosmic stare.

I can taste the tumbleweeds as they dance along the edge of the vineyard. I can smell your amusement, for I have been locked inside myself for so many days.

Weeping for the Mockingbird to come and find my dwelling place and spare me wings for I need to take flight in this ever-present air of melancholy.

I toss and turn in lavender dreams with sun ripened surprise and hope soon he might hear my call. Tears are splinters and my limbs are rocks in a vacant valley of wondering souls. I loathe the thought of loneliness being a friend.

Resting my weary bones upon the ledge of a sea of a thousand laments stretched out before my eyes. One touch of your hand sets me on an adventure on this everlasting emotional trial. Surrender guilty, I would, if it would bring your boots to my door.

For the sycamore has no comfort in this distance and her leaves laugh hysterically to see myself in ruins. I chuckle in the wind, remembering this is what I deserve.

I heard the forecast calls for winds from the north east today.....I'm just not going to be able to sail.......

......today.

Sandalwood

I articulate, no unsung lines
A curve around my lips
Refused, dignity has its price
I still follow your beacon.

Gentle radiance, magnificent proportions
I force myself to witness
My heart pours out in scales and fractions
Melodies are my words
Your name is my key

A touch, a tear falls
Lust, justified false hood
My heart is weeping,
Chipped at the seams.
Showered, your crown of moonlight
Daisies in the wind;
Perplexed.

Glance to the east, I to the west
Impression, your eyes see my soul
Heart feels my hunger
Hands find their way
Preoccupied.

Identification transformed
A puzzle, am I?

Enchanted Lucky Fool

Corner piece stranded under the light
Do I question...?
Will you come find me?

Good-bye
Eyes lower, lips quiver, heart shatters
I remember you
Dark eyes, olive skin, immaculate
Foremost thought
First time I saw your face...
...Sandalwood.

Somber

Can you hear my voice?
It was the red wine that brought out the sparkle in your eye.
Hoping that it was my presence.
Yellow oil based paint spread throughout the room, in hopes
That the mood would unfold.
Radicals on Madison Avenue, the wind muffled the voices
And my heart was still.
Strawberries hand dipped in chocolate in your honor,
An array of imported wines, distilled to perfection
For the way that you could've loved me.
Bells and soldiers line up for the defeat, tangible
They seemed.
Your shrine polished ever so delicately, lead stones draped
In rosary, my chin held high.
Immaculate,
As you strolled through the vestibule,
Hands filled with the separation,
My heart weighs heavy.
Ink placed to the paper,
I tremble.
Your signature so rare, bewilderment over comes.
I scribble.
We say good-bye.

Speechless

Jaunt.
Mindless entry into a mind field
Living out the dreams of the forgotten
Pencil in my statue
Blacken my eyes
Oil paint my heart
I am speechless

Stormy Weather

A Rumble...
A crease in the sky;
In my head,
Hearing the breath of a distant love.
Fearing the detriment,
Demise is covered in chocolate,
Another bite...
I indulge!
Air is stale;
Spring is bringing the faint laughter,
Humiliation is at my side
Determination has fallen behind.
Do you remember me?
Liquid ice is formed around the lips,
Hurricane's dropping by for a visit.
A evening so tranquil,
Eternal!
Forgive the circle that binds;
They all have flown away,
Left here standing in a monkey sea.
Knee deep in tears, salt stained
Dried to the core,
Forgive my language
Pottery is an expression
Repressed and stationary.
I lie my heart at your feet,
Bury me in your skin

Enchanted Lucky Fool

Forcing my lungs to breathe your breath
I swim into your eyes.
I fear!
Sleep is peaceful, for you're my darkness
I tail along the with stormy weather...
Do you remember me?

Strangers

We walk around the house as if we are strangers
No touch
No speak
No comfort
Four weeks and and six days have I noticed the decline in the
amount of romantic glances, the never-ending hugs and the light
in your eyes ablaze.

Funny in a way, thoughts all point to this is our honeymoon
period, most people say at least six months after you move in,
then you learn to live your life.

I am not ready for the honeymoon to be over. I am not ready
to live with short lines spoken, no affection returned....That I
am not ready.

Funny, how we used to be not bored when we are in each
other's company, and I still feel that way.

I guess in every relationship there is a person who loves too
much and one who love's too little, I thought we were going to
be different. I thought we were going to reach for the stars and
set world records on fire...

We still can. I have a world beyond your wildest dreams of
love, emotions and good times, but you hinder me when you
don't speak, don't touch and show no comfort.

I can't do this alone. I need your help and you guidance and
assistance to make this relationship work...help me to help you

Tell me when things are wrong in your mind, tell me when
things are not so right. Do you know what an open door of
communication does for me and what it would do for you.

Until we overcome that bridge, we will still be strangers walking through the same rooms, wondering what is wrong with the other person and then in time, we won't wonder anymore, since there will be nothing left to wonder about, cause it all will be gone.

Clock

I am stale
I hear the clock tick
Minutes, seconds
Hands move slowly
Destine to tell my hour
I am hurled over
Disgust

I am a prisoner
A clock of harsh words
A misery that is overbearing
A conscious that forgets the right
And commits the wrongs

Walk down the hall
Trot up the stairs
I wait for peace
Please
Come and find me.

Under a Sheet of Grey

Looking inward, not getting anywhere...
Where have I gone?
Feeling isolated in this phone booth on the East Side of town...
No compass to guide me along.
Falling into traps that have been set along this path of thorns;
I breathe in;
I breathe out.
Tomorrow seems like looking through the forest through the
trees...
No end,
No beginning.
I feel a swell in my heart;
Smoke that invades my body.
Stones and flint is all that run from my mouth;
Could I be so unkind?
Looking for Alice and the tea party;
I need a drink to ease my throat;
The lion was out again.

Too many lines to be read between the words you say....
Never knowing the right verbs or adjectives;
They just fade away.
I stand a mute on a tall mountain...
Grasping from the latitude.
Is this home?
Voice is what I have and one I don't use...
For only a small repair has been done today.

I hear the wheels as they spun out of sight...
Engulfing the words that were spoken.
Do I stand?
Seemly to hit another root in this path of thorns,
I falter.
A heart aches and shall bruise;
Although, nothing falls from my lips....
Just the sound of my breath.

I could begin with another logic intellectual statement...
Just closing the door on myself again.
Feeling pity on myself does not comprehend;
Strong, determined and closed mined....
I fall.

I try and compute your feelings;
Just as a mainframe would data...
Except, my heart gets in the way.

Looking on from the dark shaped world of life....
I pretend that there is comfort on the other side;
No reason...Just reassurance....
I thought.

Thoughts will always hinder what I feel, say and do...
Sometimes the writing is on the wall...
Yet, the paint is vibrant...
It's blurring the edges of my mind...
Forgetting is all in the plan,
The painted dessert has not been a friend.
I hear Jezebel asking me favors...
I hear Jerusalem calling me back...

Enchanted Lucky Fool

Which way do I turn?
I have no wood for me to fall on...
I have no book to guide me;
Just the sound of the winds in my heart.
Good judgement doesn't always come in pairs;
Sometimes the weather is cold;
I feel the frost and Jack is laughing at me, again.

Dark tunnels and vast lands;
I dream that haunts my existence;
Anybody out there?
I'm a sponge that weathers the storms;
Then cleans out the fire.
Many rooms and holes fill me emptiness I feel inside...
I don't need anybody to understand.
Rain can turn to snow and still life could be a vacation...
When do I leave for the plane?

Time is up.
I missed the flight from nowhere to somewhere...
Why am I still standing on this platform?
I've lost the game and won the faults...
I'm high now.
Look around and the world seems to laugh...
I must have a green egg on my shoulder.
Nobody knows the secrets people hide;
Whether it be physical or social...
I'm not a dictator that happens to fall from grace...
Flesh and blood when the wolves are out at night.

Everything is perfect;
Only when everything is in it's place.

Torturing myself over defeat;
Crazy as the next one.
I still will never comprehend the feelings that fill my head;
I could walk on water;
Yet, what's the use when there's no one beside you…
To guide…
To triumph…
To laugh.
So, I end my journey in the same dead place where it started…
My feet don't move;
My lips still stationary…
I continue along this path of thorns…
Never knowing when the fog will cease…
Never knowing when the smoke I inhale is too much…
Always will stand under the Sheet of Grey.
Just….the sheet of Grey.

Untamed

Fiction.
Not a stitch of truth to be told
Lied under the iron weights of promises…
Noteworthy,
Your voice quivers when you bellow
Stalwart, as you whisper in harmony
Wanting not to forge for your enlightenment…
Your trust gives me nothing to gain
Victory is all seen in your vision…
Loathing is escaping mine.
Wound me with the verbs you shall cast
I live not for sentiments, yet
Only for dreams
Rage is here, storms begin…
Answers…
Listen to the rain.

.

VOID

A cold chill just stirred my heart
Filled with tenderness, I let a demon arise in my throat
For I have forsaken identity with liberty
Where shall I fade?

Cruel, thoughtless and trivial
A mind numb in distinction to careless behavior
Do I deserve to be blissful?

Left skid marks
A road of uncertainty
Insanity will lurk up from behind
I dwell on voids and mishaps
Who shall I turn to?

My heart will shatter
My life resemble worthlessness
And I will drown in bitter sorrows
And then...
Left with nothing but a lonely soul
This is what I deserve!
And this is what I shall receive...

White Seat of Passion

Soiled window sill

Reflection in a glass sky
Necessity, a wish of laughter
Outcry
Sun drapes my mood in yellow
Spectrum of broken hearts
Layers unravel.

Pulverize
Breath, shredding the linens
Eyelash upon the cotton
Hear my song, no?
Perfection is desolate
Fractured, the china is somber
I sing my song

Constuients
A flock of equivocation
Names outlined in seeds
Wildflowers are for the pretty boys
Burrow of mud, my home
Sanctuary,
A bliss of fortune
Undermined in determination
I sit, face the west
Tears streaming south
I forgive you.

Winter tears

Pull back the reins
Water is solid
I descend into sequence
Apprehensive of the fall

Skin,
Silky as the sheets
We slept for hours
Our locks of hair interwoven
We shared one breath

You gaze into my eyes
Stained with your name
Cheeks, rose-red
Sliding your finger down the side of my face

Eyelash left upon my chest
I claim artifact
Rays of light rose across my forehead
I wave good bye

Lilies will cry for roses
Sobs echo from within
Bury my head in satin
I shed my winter tears

Your eyes

Questioning your eyes,
How they resemble melancholy.
Caliginous clouds around your halo,
As the wind pierced the right cheek.
Shifting an eyebrow,
As to block a distant memory.
Are you thinking of a past love affair?

Your eyes shimmer,
The sunset upon your shoulder,
Glitter fades to an endless sea of black.
Purposely surrounding yourself
In an aura that will not pass in time.

Lips stationary, rounded face
Just a mirror of the moon.
Shielded by the conditions that weigh
In your heart;
You abruptly turn away.
An ocean, you may hold along
With all its contents.
Still hanging foolishly,
Watching time pass.

Darrell J. Gawlik

Minutes churn to hours,
Hours will become years.
Still, so vibrant
Hanging in the solitude you prefer.

Your eyes,
Giving away to the souls that have passed.
Mystery lurks as sorrow dwells,
Fascinated by the simplicity
Of an arched brow.
For the face that makes people smile,
Only still;
Makes me cry.

Chapter Three

Piss and Vinegar

Beautiful Deception

I shall wander;
Destine to the mountain peaks;
Valley's of greenery and foliage;
Streams that meet the tides;
Birds fly carelessly.
DECIEVED AM I!

My love,
Bitterness waits in your giving;
Pouring my heart in a glass;
You shattered with your fist.
A reflection on remorse;
I heed your image.

Vanish your love into a well;
A well of demise and self loathing;
A bottomless pit of emptiness;
A colorless painting.

Darrell J. Gawlik

Want your love?
Certainty has fallen;
Misled is a game;
For you are wise, my love!
I shall strike a rock into my heart;
Pour the blood from my veins;
I will be rending from you.

Bitter

Am I feeling as death as crawled upon me?
Bones are brittle and every movement creates energy
And then I fall to the ground.
Bitter.
That I am.
I looked for the colors hidden inside of happiness;
All I find is the gray lining.
I am on a blissful road that sometimes is tragic.
Can someone or something,
Urgently aid in my sorrow!
Don't throw me to Hades;
I can cry no more.

You take my hand and grace your cheeks;
I fall apart.
Say you love me, damn it!
My words fall like rain against your face.
My knees filled with water;
My hands tremble with every fiber.
I fell in love.

I shutter to the wind, as you chuckle.
You find my wounds humorous.
My bleeding heart unforgiving.
How dare you touch my lips and quiet my words.
How dare I pour my emotions into your bucket?
Only for you to throw me them in a well.

Darrell J. Gawlik

Am I going crazy?
Leave me be;
An let me rest inside my inner circle of peace.
I feel so quiet there.
Content is a feeling of forever...
And that is all I ever wanted.

Black-Veil

A hateful hate lurks deep down inside my soul;
Screaming;
I want to crucify my entire existence;
Betrayed;
Taking the lines I have spoke;
Advantage, you have taken;
Disciplined;
I stutter to defend my honor.
Forgive your ignorance;
I will not!
Assistance to the light;
I will not help forge.

Desolated;
Aiming to conquer of selves;
An army of untrained soldiers heading for the field;
A battle with no victory.
Blood starts to shed;
Tears start to spill;
A halt, you will find.
Yet, insisting to move forward;
Stabbing, betraying and pain;
You have inflicted unto me.
A reason;
Why I shall never forgive you.

You have damned me all these years;
Silence.

Captivity, you hold my shimmer from your constituents;
Isolating my being;
From a rekindling friendship.

Admiration.
Admiration for a simple fact;
You gleam at others as they burn in a hell; that
You have signified as their destiny.
Strength, I admire;
But I;
I, the one who speaks n tongue
I, who expresses the passion;
I, who speaks for who I am.
Confusion haunts my wickedness;
In which you lack.
Who am I?

Weakened by your presence;
Too weak to battle your hate;
Too weak to struggle with your ego;
Too weak to confront your veracity.
Reversing the mirror;
A mysterious covert;
Who's that on the other side, Alice?

A façade;
Inside you tremble;
Ultimate fear;
A fear that has brought you demise and shame;
The human that you truly are.
Banish your façade into the dust;
Let your beauty rise above all;

The world isn't bound in scripture;
Seamed in nature;
Flourished with love.
Storms will rage and the sea stain your cheeks with salt;
Let your inner self rise;
Let it rise above the endless hate society has pressured;
You to seize.

Terrified.
Realization of lifting your black-veil provides your weakness;
Exposed to the irony of your destiny.
A emerald statue,
You once stood erect;
Podium, eulogy in hand.
Disgusted with envy;
I loved you.

Needed you.
You weren't there.
Never once did you lend your silver glove;
The rivers raged in my face;
Kettles boiled in my mouth;
Noticed my defeat;
You did not.
Blackened eyes;
Dark as miner's coal;
Filled with water…
You glared over them…
You glanced over me.

Remembering.
Grass was green in the pastures;

Friendship never had the smell stale bread;
One and one equals one;
Combined in sprit, mind and resolution.
Crying waves of laughter;
Laughing at the skies;
Surrender of the day.
Conversing in tones and pitches;
Team of two bodies;
Collided at flame of brotherhood.
Remembered.

Descending to the ground;
The shell broke;
The waves settled;
The pastures died.
Forces that bind;
The witches stacked their claim;
Once more.

We have approached our destination.
Acquaintance, merely passing pedestrians.
Forgiveness;
A language I will never comprehend.
Forgetfulness
A process that haunts me.
Leave;
Thoughts, emotions, ideas and dreams;
Is simply a character lost in my mind?
Just a simple thought before I turn to go;
A apart of my being;
Long time ago.

Cupid

Creature that roams my head;
Hidden in crevasse;
A cloud in the distance
An illusion of no shape
From afar you won't see I.

Unclose, I am utterly invisible;
Romantic lines, I have none.
Beautiful swan song, I have none.
Touched with elegance,
Propelled by your grace;
Stationary in a frame of time.

Lend me your voice, I offer my throat
Verbalize one spoken word;
'Tis this what I dread?
A glacier from the north.
Hinder my limbs.
I am a statue of love and devotion.

Wings are torn;
Arrow bent.
Waiting to be healed once more.
Use dialogue in metaphors;
Speak of nothing but heavenly words;
Assume I am tangible.
Touch me as if I consume space.

Darrell J. Gawlik

Boring into your eyes;
Desperate to see my reflection;
Mirrored is a source of emptiness;

Be on your way,
Leave me to rest.
No hope;
No Love;
Just a hollow chest.

Deafening Secret

Heard the whimper of the willow
Yesterday, Today and tomorrow
I fail
Poised to the nines
Drunk on strawberry liquor
Raise your glass
Make the toast
Black-n-blue, eyes that wept
Your absences is feared
Drowned sorrow
Liquorish smiles
I dive into your eyes
Fists, screams and ravished smirks
Speech impaired, spell in breath
Rings exchanged, vows spoken
Holy is the lie,
Oath is the lock!
Leave the veil
Consume a rose
A journey you step forth
Early grave is your wrath.
I kneel,
Kiss your wounds
…And say good-bye.

Dreaming Thoughts

I close my eyes, letting my mind wander the city streets in a dazed confusion. Helplessly, I focus on an object too far from my tunnel vision. The dream is gone.

Pigments of purplish reds flash across my vision. A figure with a mesmerizing face and strong hands frees my vivid soul. Who are you to judge me? Why when I dream you come to me?

My soul keeps searching, yet only in dreams am I alive. Reality has no hold on what tomorrow will bring fourth for me, nor does it prove that there is destiny. Maybe I despise life and all it's multitude of creations and its biology. Effortlessly, I let my soul seek hidden treasured mountains where enchanted ruby's fall into the grasp of my hands; while they fall threw my fingers and drop to the bottomless soil. Is this happiness?

I dig deep into the dirt, my hands raw with the constant pounding of the earth to my flesh. I just want to wash away the pain of struggle. I want to drown out my misery and throw away despair. Why am I not strong enough to face my sorrow and find tranquillity in those that deem me special?

I hurt.

I cry streams of tears in hopes that someone will come and wipe them away. My cheeks red with bitterness and stained with salt. I will not rise above this negative reinforcement. I throw my hands to the sky.

Never-ending questions, haunting my thoughts. They dwell inside this forsaken and battered heart. Thoughts rearrange the furniture in my head and throw forbidden kisses off the stairwell into a swamp of pure vile and poison. I am content in these thoughts of mystical places.

I have thrown my words to the ground in hopes the fairies would pick them up. My words have no meaning. Wisdom is the facade I hold the mirror up to as I swallow the lies that fall from my black and blue lips.

Force your lips against mine in a passion that would break my halo. I want your lies and your dishonesty to fill my mouth. I want your empty sighs and your fake groans to empty out into my body. Don't say you love me! Use this body as you would a rag doll. Scorn me and throw me back into my pit of weakness. I am at home here.

Do you hear the war that grows inside my mind? Not understand that I want to love your face and your knowledge; I want to be whole and free. I want to see green once more and to be able to lift my head up high without the voices telling me indifferent. Will you help me?

I am just having thoughts on how you could have saved my heartless body. If you had looked to the surface of my lust and the spectrum of my realm, you would have seen the beauty that I would have held for you. But you didn't.

Remembering the restless nights while somber was far from my eyes. I realize that I will forever dwell in this house of darkness and despair. The endless lies and hatred you have handed to me permanently will plague me.

Your lips brushed against mine and I awoke.

They were thoughts,

...Just thoughts.

Fool

Walls smothered, burgundy drapes outlines
Olive green
Photographs poised in
Harmonious sequences, detailed rustic frames
Smeared golden leaf.
Layered texture, orderly perfection
Is an art,
Tapestries dance, a breeze redefined
Parallel lines, eyes reflected shapeless stares.
Geometrical confines, sped through a lifeless room.
Hexed.

Hovering, a still life as to disregard my shadow
Angelic thoughtlessness.
Isolation crept along a virtual spine,
Needful stroke,
Gone stale
Winter affirmed
Breathing abjection, absent configuration
For which is demanded.
Forbidding youth, peering through
Stained glass on which has been built.

Five fingers extended, soothing the wind…
I salute freedom.

good-bye

At will, dwelling in an effortless
Cubical, no hindsight
Energetic, through a wire hinged jaw.
Dramatization,
A child's game
In a stretched, concealed
Battered mind.
A winged angel perched,
Immaculate structure
Draped in white linen.
Sweltering darkness eclipsed,
Abides farewell.
Muscles tormented, howling pain
Love displays its final ado.
Tenderly among the mist, a sullen sky
Hurricane swells, lungs tighten
I wept.

Hunt

A soul hardens with each line you don't recite
Honey lingers
As you grace the stale air
Your breath, your undertone
Brutal as the winds in December
Moments not long ago
A remembrance
Youthful.
Beautiful.
I once experienced
Two hours after paradise
Path of lilacs turned brown
Icicles form as you pass by
Touch, none for you to offer
Ugliness with stroke of gray
Clouding a view of wonderful
Will you ever love again?

The stench of loathing
The crust upon your lips
A blank stare
Monotone speech
A black bird cries your name
You let me out to hunt again
Dwell in your decaying walls of solitude.

Jealously

Tunnel vision, limbs smoldering
Scent of isolation, haunting bones
Beneath the canopy...
Draped vines, seductive fruits, succulent raspberries
I taste the wine.

Liquid surface, rocks between my toes
Drifting sand, you close my eyes
Dreaming, color's harmonious
I touch the sky.

Fall behind, nowhere to be seen
Walls so thick, space divides
Mustard paint, granny smith apple green tints
Diving, belly first
I forgive.

She, with desire triggered
Unfastened buttons, tie the lace
Underworld Goddess, awaken
Claws of venom, mouth of deceit
Go with her, I lie.
Façade takes shape, you lie.
Deep waters...
Who's left standing?

Darrell J. Gawlik

Hands lose grip, tears fall
Lifeline vanished, a wrinkle appears
Terrible hours, bitter pain
Lifeless joy, I wait.
A moment dies, visions deceptive
Summer rain sheds it's skin, open my eyes
Looking down, a puddle
…and my reflection.

Jezebel

As I plunge to my narrow wooden bed;
I take along with me, hopes and fears.
My mind is stationary, the water I tread.
The earth is soiled with cold salty tears.

No more shall I strive for unanswered love;
You drape my being with shame and demise.
Once you perched like a white winged dove;
Presently, you're no more than bark of the old oak tree.

Please, don't weep over my forgotten, broken heart;
Let me rest into the world of the unknown;
My fountain of youth has disintegrated;
Cover me with dirt, affix the stone.

I was bound in your rapture; now I'm free;
I cannot forgive you; leave my heart be.

Letters

Let the pen flow across the lines;
Shade in the tolerance of disguise.
Place your hand on your head...
Are the words true?

Can I hold you to the ink?
To the loneliness you describe.
Your hands tremble; I see the swirls...
Your combing your knowledge;
With verbs and nouns.

Skeptical,
An eyebrow raised...
Speak of tomorrow; you don't trust
Yesterday,
Full of hope; a half pint of guilt;
Wounded by the shape of the O's;
Doubting the doted I's.

You tell stories on of love, truth and honesty;
Your letters tell stories;
Stories of forgotten bias;
And roaming fields.
I tear the paper....
All I hear is lies being burned....
Just like your letters.

SKY

How you linger in my desolate state of mind,
Forbidding enjoyment of fruitfulness.
Farewell, you abide me in steel tongue,
Although you traipse in frivolous dreams.

Breath dampens my forehead,
Eyes ablaze in fury,
For I am bewildered with rage.
The sight of your ghostly complexion,
Brings ill to my dawns,
And anguish to the dusk.
I loathe your being in a masquerade
Of cowardly lions and grotesque wounds.
Despising all that you touch,
Wishing your falter,
I have no shame.

Rekindled any form of truth,
Do you dare muster?
Jealous of my nature, a beast of
Bounty and slight perfection,
As you dwell in your house
Of hollow wood, cursed stained glass and
The smell of disappointment.

Wanting your calendar days, in my shoes
For which you have no control.

Knots if your throat, for the rope has
Grown too tight, and no handyman at your side.

A color washed with your letters, tormented
Are the walls that have been splashed.
Manipulate with your twisted elegance,
Scatter your currency where ego's lay.
For no soul will be true, no words will comfort
Your false security.

Never living to feel the honesty of love,
Just remembering a day or year,
For affection was delivered when you paid.
Deserved is this hole of sorrow,
Engraved with your name,
And I, the scripture.

One day,
Dreams will cascade with light
While days linger worrisome free.
The guilt shall exit my body,
And I,
Will love without knowing
That once he loved you.

Sonnet I

Three long years I cried over your unloved soul;
    You deceived my heart and tore it in two.
My world used to be blood red; now it's blue.
    You made my eyes turn as black as coal;
You're the witches favorite trademark; her mole.
I once found your love was kind and true
    The love that you had is now far and few.
Your beauty has gone away; now you're a troll.
Take your affection; throw it to the ground.
    I don't want it in my chest anymore.
So, lead your tenderness to the bounds of the earth;
    Don't let your dreadful spirit linger around.
Close your portal; shut your blood stained door.
The most hateful day for me, was your birth.

Unworthy

My heart lies beneath the canopy of snow
Blood still pumping, yet the warmth is gone
I think that love still lies there
Where is yours?
I cry to you
The salt stains my face.
You'll never know how sorry, I am.

I wished upon the brightest star each dusk
Praying that I was worthy of your love
For the smoke blurred my vision!

I yearn to be moral
And to have a sense of life
The good book, never lied
Blessed with the Holy Spirit
Therefore, I shunned
Trying to forget the word
Feeling....unworthy.

I don't know how to justify pain;
For pain is all I have felt in these last hours,
Playing in three's when two is all we have;
These tears might stop with time;
And the stains will fade into my pours,
As yours will the same.

Enchanted Lucky Fool

Learned a lesson;
Don't give what others want;
The tears will flow again.
Life could never be the same without your presence,
Love and dignity.

When your soul is near my soul;
And our hearts collide as one;
When our mountains crumble;
When our well is a dustbowl;
And when we are both clean;
We are one
United.

Yet, for a substance breaks my heart
Each inhale steps me further from you;
Each word that you speak
When the smoke is running through your blood
Are lifeless.

Starting over;
Brand new
Is the wish that I dream;
You needing me,
I needing you...

As long as the substance stays in our union;
Mountains will crumble;
Our well will run dry;
And we will become two.

Darrell J. Gawlik

I have learned passages,
Those only float in a bottle,
You are my sea…

I could never see you on a plane;
Nor with someone else's breath in your mouth
Although, if you change;
I change.
Never wanting to force a path for one
Yet, it breaks me in two
When I see blood in your eyes
Vowing to change;
Begging for the same

Remissness about the life we once lived;
How the fresh grasses smelled;
Days lasted forever.
Kisses that went on for miles;
And hugs so suffocating.

If we go on living the same past hours;
I can feel the earth shake;
Are liberty will crumble
And both
You and I
Are unworthy….
Of each other.

Vanishing

Tales unravel,
Poe's mysteries bejeweled
Knowing how my feet are planted.

Truth drizzling,
Hesitant to pour a cup overflowing.
Falsity,
Skillfully packaged between the molars;
A vacant remedy can conquer.
Was your love secure enough?

An altered name,
Systematized body,
Sorrow will extinguish my song, not soul.
Secure a tender passion,
Char to ashes.
Sentences splashing against the wall,
Cast your lies to the beasts of the night.

I hung your fruit from my vine,
A stalwart trunk and loved, from faith
Jupiter is strong,
I shall weep no longer.

Your presence no longer required
Heading west.
Vanishing,

Darrell J. Gawlik

Final footnotes;
Existing, you shall roam earth..
As I go on living.

Chapter Four

Enchanted

Moment and Patient

Stains have been left upon my heart from the absence of your presence;
Sometimes out of bounds;
A little to the left…
More to the right;
A medium dwelling place for sorrow…am I.
I lunge to the ground only to taste the bitterness of the earth…
Is there no wine left here in the cellar?
Questions haunt my source of inner displacement;
Answers hidden deep inside the concrete walls;
Do I hunt for you in the castle?
Do I search for you in the lilac gardens of forbidden desires…?

Rain pours down from the sky;
It falls on my wounded heart only to add comfort.
Thunder and lightening collide unavailing a moment in time.
A moment so pure and blissful…
A moment wrapped in the arms of love…
A moment when I saw your chiseled features shine through the crisp
morning air.
A time when you were near.

Darrell J. Gawlik

Do I drain my body of self-pity and surrender to temptation?
Do I stand proud of who I am and what I want to become?
Heaven to the west;
Still my sleep is not restful.
Dreams so vivid filled with hunger, anger and rage.

Cupid is standing above me;
I steal his bow and arrow in spite.
Running with the wind, hoping it will take me west...
Winding over green hills, mountains and across lakes;
It gives out before the last stretch;
I give in.

Exhausted,
Energy depleted from my body.
I look to the midnight sun and wish upon the stars...
Desperation fills my thoughts on how to get to you...
Patience is the answer that lights the sky.
Patience is my enemy!

A heart full of misery until that heavenly day my eyes meet yours...
Now, I wait to your east, you to my west
...Yearning to be set free.

Night

Peer through the thicket,
Moon glow on the east
Beacon in the west
Orchids circle around your feet
Shakespeare flowing from your mouth
Every syllable falls from your lips
I gaze.

Rose red outlines your cheeks, you blush
Distinct stature, you tower above
Pick an apple, pinch the peach
a soul lucid, as I dive into your eyes
swimming in afterglow, bathe in the moonlight
hours after hours in the midst of unmasked smirks
I call your name,
Will you hear me?

True Fable

A true fable, life story
Whispered from your lips
Canopy of snow
Fallen across my chest, I said
When did the tree tops shutter to the wind?
I ask
You lie face down in the roots
I turn away

Bizarre, unsettling is this dream
You spoke
Watching the quiver of your lips
I gaze
Melting down, I cry with the storm
Your hand embraces mine
Quick moments, unforeseen nakedness
We each bare our souls
You whimper, I cradle your face

Touching the earth, many moons disappeared
Brave the storm
In distress, you wave good-bye
I flutter for words:
Adoration, enchanting, perfection
Charmed, you thought
Looking to the iced twigs

Enchanted Lucky Fool

Time is virtuous, you whisper
Love, I sign to you
As you leave your footprints in the snow.

We Danced

As the cold Winds blew from the north then to the east;
Air swept through your blackened hair.
You summoned the courage and the strength while sheltering me from
the storm.
Too many years;
Too many days pass while my energy is depleted from my mouth to
yours.
Breathless and daring as daisy's painted against a hard sheet of a painter's
canvas,
My heart fell for you.
Twilight falls and the North Star winks at my being;
A signal of approval from the heavens.
Can I intertwine between your lifelines?
Honor me,
Let me be the energy that beacons from your body.
I learn through your thoughts;
I dream through your ideas;
And live through your wisdom..

Searching over hand and foot;
Wandering aimlessly and alone;
Your hand touched, and the flowers bloomed once more.
Rivers and steams filled with life once more;
And on the seventh day,
you were born.

Enchanted Lucky Fool

Lend me the wisdom of how to keep showering your beauty with rose
pedals, offering white sand at your feet.
I feel no obligation to surrender kindness and compassion;
Your smile is my reward.

Raging storms, tears that spill over;
My hand shall protect you.
These simple thoughts flow in me.
When the times comes and the winds sweep onc of us away,
We both could go on living,
knowing we'd meet again.
…And fall in love once more.

Breathe

No single thought embedded
A swirl of colors falls to the canvas
Distinguished, reds yellows and greens
My eyes fall short
For the ending may not be a dream

Clenched teeth, stargazed eyes
Where is your beacon tonight?
Packaged am I underneath your arm
Your torso glides against mine
Lips grazing fingertips, anticipation overwhelming
Captive by the scent of the night,
I wait for the morning.

Locks of hair intertwined,
An eyelash lies upon my cheek
Your sweet smell lingers, thick as molasses
My eyes are heavy, your grip is persuasive
Engulfed in the midst of desire
You ask what I am thinking
Spellbound as a loon, stretched as taffy
A single thought left hanging from my mouth
In a bed full of cotton, a lad at my side

Remember to breathe......

Daydreaming

A sunset speaks of love
Laying arm in arm with you.
Violet whispers, green embraces
As is full of hope;
As I steal a kiss

Maple trees sway in the breeze
Covering our bodies intertwined
A blanket of leaves, one falls to your shoulder
Comfort hidden in the winds from the east

Sipping your gourmet coffee;
Stirring my green leaf tea
While romance echoes from the harbor.

Make-a-wish
Make-a-wish
Make-a-wish
…For me

Daydreaming by your side, a book of poems in my hands
Oil paints and a sheet of canvas stretched out where you lie

You whisper; "I love you"
Time is near to close up a momentous day;
I smile at the thought
Home is by your side, where I lay.

Fervent

Hours,
I name each second from the words you have spoken
Evergreen frosted tips, yellow mist sunsets, Appalachian dreams
I am frantic.
Crazed as the Loon, speckled as the barn yard owl
Your presence, I fear to want
Yet, I cling to every syllable
You apprehend whimsical magic,
I harvest your brilliant brown eyes

Chaotic, my intellect misjudged
Reasoning abandoned, discretion unveiled
I am toppling into your arms
Your glance clenches my heart from across a room;
A Room lined in white linen, drapery covered with orchids
A rose, near my heart

I, utter no words of melancholy, a code of silence
I flourish in pentameter sonnets, Shakespeare is splendid
Wooing with letters, dotted I's and crossed T's, symbols and ink
When voiced, the speech collapsed
Reddened are my cheeks
Seep down into my soul;
A murky lagoon, mortar roads, pebble walls,
Dense forestry with a mindful mystery
Do you dare follow?

Enchanted Lucky Fool

Haunting looks and famished fixations
Desire, do I read from your lips?
Tranquillity, defined in your embrace
I dwindle like the flame, a fearless wind blows
Smothered, your emotions ignite my passion
I fall, with hesitation.

Arms length, here I would just stay;
You devour chocolate, while I watch and crave.

How I loved you

Oh…
How I loved you,
How you didn't see me,
The way I wanted you to.
Feelings warmed my heart
When you weren't around.

Oh…
How I loved you.
I didn't need signs,
Nor a letter of justification,
I just knew.

In the rain

I remember it.
Rays of light battering down from the heavens;
All I wanted was you.
Vinyl on the table, turning loose my desires;
I still feel your pulse against mine.
Loving every part of your skin;
Spider web was I.
Complex, broken, shattered in the wind.
Directions included, so I thought;
Yet, I was dyslexic;
Blurring the edges of the knife;
I faltered upon the stage;
Hoping Hamlet wouldn't see my façade.
Breeze took you east;
I perched myself in the same oak tree…
Just waiting…
Waiting for the wind to change.

…just linger

…linger
numb, is my mind
a brush on my neck
as you breathe

…linger
cascade across the skyline
skylark in the midst
distance, I watch

…linger
eyes, fixated on lips
tender are your words.
your face, crowds my mind

…linger
stories flow, a voice so secure
remembrance, a hundred minutes past
R's and L's captured, I smile.

….linger
for I may forget to speak
caught in your shadow
I hide under your chin

…just linger
summon, Strawberry Jack

Enchanted Lucky Fool

proposed, aura of Jupiter
in a world so perfect....
We just linger.

Lake Memory

Wind
In the geometry realm
Glides over every fiber
Cracker barrel, rolling waves
The scent of musk
Can you forgive my ignorance?
For the sea urchins have chimed
Mesmerize
By the chill of your shoulder
I lay in adolescent bewilderment
Intertwined in limps
Heaven only in breath
I shall return.

Loved

Breathing,
Fixated, as if it were the last breath.
Welcoming a past,
Admiring misfortunes;
Giving thanks for a hand to hold.

Friend,
A pillar for which I lean upon,
A tower that shall shed
No tears,
For we have shed enough
For two lives.

Cheer
In memory,
Pour wine
In thought,
A toast to our laughter.
Hear my voice
Coming from your heart.
Remembered;
Not in being
Yet, in soul.

Understood
I was loved.

ONE THOUGHT

Slur your words, for I know what you speak of
Tempting, forbidden and heaven will follow
I love playing in the covers with you…

RETURN TO SENDER

I tug,
You push
Where do I stand?

Ghostly,
Haunted mist dwelling within.
Moon in Scorpio;
How dare you affix your stone!
Dreadful lonely nights,
Solitary is my reward;
For I am losing at love.

Perfection, bottled and sealed
Stretched along the shoreline.
Envisioned you and I;
Warmth crushing against our skin;
Hands intertwined
Eyes reaching for the future;
Hearts accelerating for each other's dreams.
A fairy tale of sorts;
Blushing of my foolishness.

Comprehend.
How could you?
The weight of love I bare for you;
Reserved to be a shadow, you the light

Darrell J. Gawlik

I remain backstage.
A universe of splendor, the main attraction is
You

Drifting on the strings of your sleeve,
Baffled, misinterpreted and bewildered
Striving for your glory.
Who must I be?
Why must I wait?

Westward winds,
A kiss placed on it's tail,
To your heart,
In hopes of no,
Return to sender.

She

She looked into my eyes and saw emptiness. A halo she built for herself in me, knowing it was cracked. Fragile and so pure, I can see her slip away a little more each day. Still, she looks deep into my eyes straining to see her reflection.

I poured her coffee and added her sugar and cream; just how she likes it. I help with her favorite dress; just how she likes it . The pinkish cotton would light up her face, and compliment her rosy cheeks.

Only words to describe her presence, elegantly beautiful..

Only if she knew that's how I felt.

She calls out my name and I spend time with her.

She is alone in this world. She grasps for attention, anyone that will pay her a moment of intrigue. Yet, not one person will come and sit by her side, except for I. I love to hold her hand and listen to her old stories and fond memories about her kids and her husband. He passed away 2 years ago. She tells stories in such detail I feel that I know him; as if I was his friend that he would spend time with and talk over the telephone.

Yet, I never knew him, nor even saw a photographic of this man. Still, I listen to her vivid stories and pretend that I am a part of her family.

I imagine how she would be as a young woman. Holding her head up high and breezing through the crowds of men at the park. She would be classy and radiant, as the sun brushed against her olive toned skin. Everyone admired her intelligence and wisdom; she would be very diplomatic.

That's how I pictured her life to be; that's how I wanted the story to go. Yet, I was wrong. She always stayed home and tended to her husband and three children. No time for walks in the park. Never enough time to be beautiful and play dress up to boost the self-esteem she lacked on the inside.

Some say she was poor, but what they didn't know is that she was rich with love. Three children and how they loved her; always picking flowers in the meadows, only to please her with the brilliant colors of spring. How she loved them back; reading books of magical places, telling bedtime stories about mystical lands of dragons and fairies. She loved her family. She would packing daddy's lunch, shower him with heavenly kisses and always had dinner for him at five till five. While everyone was at school and work she would scrub the floors, wash their clothes and make their shack a lovely home. She had love, which was her pay. That's all she had to offer and all she had to give never thinking about her self. Now, they are all gone.

Sometimes I wonder what she thinks, as she is silent waiting for the next story to brew. I wonder if she thinks, "Why did I do all of that for?"

Knowing her that never crossed her mind. "It was time worth spent" I think would be her answer. Maybe one day I will ask her, then again maybe I won't.

One afternoon she held my hand real tight after a very long involved story about her kid's death and as she finished she looked deep into my eyes and sighed. A look of contentment and joy spread across her wrinkled face. She squeezed my hand ever so tightly and closed her eyes.

Stunned for a moment. Just rehashing that beautiful look across her face and not realizing she had just let my hand go. Her hand was just lucid and soft gently resting against my arm. I looked over to her, fearing her eyes were still closed.

"I can go now." she muttered as a soft gaze covered her eyes.

I nodded with approval and she died. I turned to look for help, wanting someone to bring her back to me. Not wanting to let go of all the stories. Fearful that I will be alone once more. I needed her as much as she needed me. Now, she was gone and I was left alone with my endless days and dreadful nights. Her beautiful hello's and hopeful good-bye's will I never her again. I sat there is disbelief, for I just lost my best friend. A friend I never would have imagined having, or caring for. All in a moment, the three years I have been coming to see her, didn't matter. Nothing mattered at his moment. All that I knew is that she was gone and I devastated from the loss.

I finally cried. I cried so hard that my stomach pained and my throat dry and the salt burned my skin. I cried for many days after that afternoon.

She taught me how to love. She taught me to look deeper into life and find the gold within yourself before you find it in anybody else. She taught me that when you love somebody, you look deep into his or her eyes and search for your reflection.

One last lesson she taught me. She taught me that it's all right to love and be loved; that's what we are here for.

She never said she loved me, but deep inside I knew....

I loved her,

...and she loved me.

Snow Day

Perpendicular creases dignify your prestige, as the light beams through the morning curtains, I watch in awe.

I think, " How long does perfection last?"

You reply, " It lasts as long as you fill my eyes."

The snow has drifted; mounds of pearly white flakes summon to their home on the ground. We watch in the warmth of candlelight. You slide to the left and take my head under your arms, as you gently place a kiss on my forehead. I turn to you for justification.

" How long does perfection last," I ask

"It lasts as long as you fill my eyes" you replied.

My heart beats with the rhythm of your favorite song, while you hum the tune in my ear. I catch each breath as you gasp the lines that have meaning.

You sing to me.

The covers positioned to our waists, snuggled deep inside the warmth of our cocoon. All is safe and silent, no words need conveyed for where we are heading. Understanding is all in the sense of movement and magic that fills our space. I wish this day to never end.

"How long does perfection last?" I ask

"It lasts as long as you fill my eyes" you reply.

Big Ben is talking. Our eyes lower, time is slowly being subtracted. Yet, bliss is wrapped up here in this bed. A picture neatly framed of Two people, two smiles and one heart. The antique frame captures a moment, yet the two people, two smiles and one heart is forever.

I want to fill your skin all day long.

I want to sit together as the snow falls on the pines, you with your coffee and I with my herbal tea, sitting in peacefulness.
"How long does perfection last?" I ask.
"Forever" you reply "as long as you are near me."

Snow Wood

Perched, hand in hand
Lingering whispers, hungry lips
Eyes a blaze, lust mingling thereafter
Hearts skipped a beat, I felt you tremble
Snow gathers around, a spectacle, we are
Leather crunching, gasping breaths
Wandering fingertips, I invite
Skin, only a luxury to touch
Delicately, grasping for the linens
Remembering the smell of your hair
Bury me in bliss….
Together, something beyond
Chocolate kisses, peppermint paddies and orange slickers
Watch the sun set,
I, in your eyes, You in mine
I am content.

Stand by You

Hidden behind your yawn
A work of art slips from your tongue
Breathing life into a voided space
A declaration of fondness for my presence
Recognizing weaknesses in the lines you feed
I am without will

Exhilaration for anticipation, your touch profound
I witness your empathy
Obstruct your identity, I will not
For I am in love with oneself
Oneself is a beautiful painting on a rustic canvas
All the while, I ache for your honest heart

Until the stars glide against my night
As the sun radiates your path of tumbleweeds
Following without hesitations
Stumbling over the rocks, bathing in seaweed
Heart in hand, breath in your lungs
I'll stand by you.

Strawberry Voice

Unruffled, precise and addictive
Each enunciation covered in chocolate
I quiver!
Breathless as each syllable falls into place
I desire your words

Floating on the Lillie pads, flexed
Muscles clenched as I linger,
A voice unheard
Notes claimed, perfection
Pitches demand acknowledgment
Persuade I, no action required
Aimless bliss, a rage unsettled
Enraptured

Summer Rain

I will bare the weight of your smile, as long as I get to see the glimmer of the sunset in your eyes. The crashing waves beat as my heart and the sand is my foundation. I lay in the rays of your light. I place a candle near the shore and wait for your return. When I close my eyes I can see the flicker of candlelight dance on your brow and I hold my breath, for the scent of hazelnut mixed with the honey falls from your lips. Is this worth the precious minutes when I forget to breathe?

I balance Red Delicious apples on top of my head. I sit in a perfect harmonious stance, back erect poised for your every word, not wanting to miss a bat of an eyelash, A curl of the mouth or a muscle twitch. I am lost in the depths of your presence. I am on a winding road and don't know whether to cross the yellow lines or slow down and stop. I speed full ahead, not knowing boundaries or if I may get lost in a dreadful desert with no water, I risk it all.

City lights block my path to your doorstep. The night owl sings a haunting tune of seduction and betrayal. I do not question the darkness; I just plant my body into the soil and wait for you to water me down. Wanting to grow in your arms and to know I am someone who dares to dream the same dream. I want the trumpets to sound and the horns to blow. I want to be the book you read each night and the light you turn on. I just want to be close to you. " We fit" you said in a whispering breath. I acknowledge your feeling, for I have felt it too. It's like the heavens light up n the 4th of July and you hear a symphony in the back of your mind. We fit, yet do we belong? A question neither you nor I have an answer. "Save it for a rainy day" I summon in my mind, then you kiss me.

You wonder if I think of you. I reply; " the stars always shine"

I have found the wild berry patch and it showers me with blissful and intoxicating smells of joy and delight. Sitting on the hush green leaves and taking it all in. Every fiber of my being screams of redemption and prosperity. That's what you have when you've found a four-letter word. A word that takes you prisoner and makes you dream upon red licorice and blooming daisies. A word that will lift you up so high and so fast and may drop you like an anchor. You could hit the bottom of the sea and then sooner or later you will swim up to the surface to breathe the fresh air once again and start all over. Those lucky fools who have the secret of love in their power will ride the waves and always have the fresh air to breathe. I want to be a lucky fool.

Let's walk out into the summer rain and dance in our bare feet. Stick out our tongues and taste the sweet of spring. Take a moment and glance around to everything that is grand. Spring is contagious. It will hollow you out and make you feel like a pedal that has just felt rain.

As I leave these words written on this page, I keep a fire in my heart. I keep a vision of you in my mind and I see your face when I look though the summer rain.

Take Me Home

Whisper your elegance,
Your thoughts betray my soul.
Ears burning from your breath,
Lips that haunt my tender neck.
Stars embellish your eyes.

Trembling, my hands
Outspoken
A face, reflected misery
Your words, inscribe my history
Proofread the lines
A story forbidden
Nothing, I fear

Fingers trace my body
Red velvet wine
Escaping your mouth
Tranquil
Mood set, grace me in rapture
Candle wax is aflame

A signature
Traced with perfume
Exquisite taste of raspberry
Calligraphy
Across my torso, I desire

Darrell J. Gawlik

Eyes capture your sensuality
A river for you to swim
Sorrow is uprooted
Discover my freedom;
Your destiny is mine.

Take me home.

Tell me a story

Tell me a story, where the fairy tale never ends
No king shall rule
And no one is wounded
I want to believe in Cinderella
And snow white can proceed

Show me a story, where the rain never falls
And the ice is never slippery
A kiss will not turn stale
Where your breath will always be felt
And Peter Pan will take my hand

Live with me in a story, where love always prevails
A fountain of bliss in every corner
Love will wrap us in its warmth,
Holding each other in the twilight
You on your chair, me on my couch
As you whisper,
I love you.

Thank-You

Walk with me;
Walk to where the water meets the sand;
Let me feel your hand in my hand;
Hoping to feel a little tenderness in your grip;
Yearning to feel your pulse against mine…
Waiting on what could be.
You smile.
I turn toward the shadows;
Fearing what I might learn from the look in your eyes.
Searching for that human touch;
That will linger when I admit defeat;
There when the world has compounded me into fragments of
glass,
There when my heart aches,
There when my little body has been worn and finally needs to
rest.
Just be there.
Your hand signifies a sense of security;
Dreams have been known to become concrete.
Possibly,
Maybe you could be the one.
One that I cry rivers to;
One that I laugh wildly with,
One that I daydream about.

Enchanted Lucky Fool

Yet, I do not love you.
Hands of time will unfold the story;
Yet, we could guide the pages as we turn them.
I elapse with time...

My lips roaming your face, hungry for a kiss.
A kiss so passionate and dark;
I melt with the candles that burn around my bed.
I want to feel that eternity with the spirituality of your kiss.

Talk to me!
Talk to me in poetic phrases;
Speak in tongue;
Whisper your passions and anguish under my covers,
Metaphor my mind until I am not able to think in equal patterns.
I want to dive into your eyes;
Your wholeness.
I need to feel each and every syllable that falls from your mouth.
Just make want to be you.
Complete my soul.
Yet, I do not love you.

My aura is in a panic;
Words are frantic.
Feelings chaotic.
Emotions charismatic.
You're an angel that has come to rescue my struggling body.
Take me to the sky;
Show me your wings.
Let's dance in the clouds and make sunshine for the world.

We will become one sex.
One.
Such a lonely number, yet the most vital feeling every known.

Isolated.
I lay here with the dew dripping down each blade of grass;
Thoughts of loneliness streak my processes;
Embracing my body;
Seemingly never-ending.
Do you believe in love?
A question that prohibits thought and ponders;
Encompassed by the answer on your lip...
I thank-you.

Beach

Cruel
Night falls over the harbor
Disheartening manipulation tingles through my fingers
Unabridged stories, neglectful fables, antique tales
A life sewn within the stitches of my jeans

Ocean crashes against my sandals
Earth presses between my heels
Serene as the reds and yellows at dusk
I bellow out a sob
A distant thunder erupting from within
I preserve my feebleness

Greeting fondly your presence
Speaking confidentially, your name
Five letters of euphoria
Occupying my space with your breath
Easing my shudder, you considerately
Place your lips to mine
"When the wind blows, it's your name I hear"
You speak ever so sweetly
"When the sun rises, it's your face I see"
You muffle my cry
"…And when the night falls, it's your heart I long for"
With a soothe stroke of your hand
Wiping my tear stained cheeks….
I know I am at home….
When I am at your side.

Beast

Seize an occasion with a sweet tongue
An appetite as crazed as the homeless, I am vengeful
Now you know how I feel

Vision substantial as I quake to the pulse of your veins
Quicken my step as I lunge for the tightrope
Only want my skin against your olive tones

Forceful it may appear as I justify my reasons
Answers oblivious to the naked eye
Never questioning the sensitivity file in my heart

Vanquish my coat of armor
Capture the doubts that surface from my mouth
Structure me whole again

Exiled has the meaning of wanting you
As needing has come to rest
I welcome with open arms...

Pinned to the pine needles with no façade in sight
I long for you body as I feel you within the night
Straight out of captivity you hunger and glow
Tame my wild heart with the desire you show
Torture with your lips that crave what they found
Spoon my body, flip me over, and turn me upside down
Forever can last 'til the next time I gaze in your eyes
Just tell me you love and don't.... Whisper good-bye.

Watercolor Whisper

Paint my world in green and caress it with a touch of yellow....
Release your emotions,
Letting them flow gently down my chest;
Burning into my primitive heart.
Light my eyes ablaze;
Turn me into diminutive specks of purified glass, while letting
my bones rust;
Yet, keeping my heart afloat alongside your body.
Wishes upon stars;
Endless prayers, a quest in doubt.
Despite my failures, you have arrived.
Turning the winds of change into winds of hope;
Your eyes shimmering wide open and your heart full of endless
wine,
I dive in.
Do I question your intentions? Do I summon endless worries
and tragic
endings?
Do I lift my eyebrows in skepticism as I swallow your precious
words that
pour from your angelic mouth?

I dance with angels;
Chant along side the demons;
I rejoice at the loveliness I have discovered in you!
You,
Reality that is cultured masterfully sculptured into a realm of

perfection.
For all I have is my canvas,
I stroke a hint of red with grace, only showing your radiant smile and how it
opens the chambers to my heart.
I stroke a hint of yellow with a delicate sweep, revealing your affection for
life and all the secrets it holds.
I stroke a hint of green with tranquillity, for all those who have not yet been
touched by your grace and your kindred spirit.
Sensitively, I paint in feelings, emotions and perfection's I sought in you;
Although, down my canvas they bleed…
They bleed down the canvas of my heart;
Those colors delicately paint a picture of one life and one love made from
two souls,
…Forever.

Weak

Feeble
Weak with love
No reformatory can chain my heart
Brush against your side
Feel the blaze
Twisted in a vice
I am at peace.
In my arms, your sanctuary
My embrace repels all hesitation
Your home.

Wilting

Picturesque
Concentrating on your exquisite form,
Perfection.
Paintings, prints and sonnets,
These are the gifts I give to you.

Wonder?

(Dedicated to Steve Lewis)

do u wonder what I am thinking as I write this letter?
do u wonder what I am thinking as I am on the other line?
do u wonder what I see when I look right into your eyes?
do u wonder how my body reacts when you brush up against me?
do u wonder what face I make when I say your name?
i wonder all these things about you.

i wonder what you think of as you wake in the morning…
i wonder what you feel as you put on your clothes…
i wonder what you think of as you look into the mirror…
i wonder what you think when you dial my number…
i wonder what you feel when you see me smile…
do u wonder these about me?

I wonder, think, in what I feel…
i never forget to think of what i thought….
do u?

About the Author

This is Darrell J. Gawlik's first collection. It has taken him eight years to complete his first book.

He lives in Rochester, New York.